A KANE COUNTY CHRISTMAS

Two Christmas Stories

Liz Adair

Ron Shook

This is a work of fiction, and the views expressed herein are the sole responsibility of the authors. Likewise, certain characters, places, and incidents are the product of the author's imagination, and any resemblance to actual persons, living or dead, or actual events or locales, is entirely coincidental.

A Kane County Christmas
Published by Century Press
496 West Kane Drive
Kanab, UT 84741

Cover image by Ron Shook
Cover design by Sai Kumar at DesignCrowd

ISBN: 978-0-9905027-2-2
Printed in the United States of America
Year of first printing: 2014

Ron and I dedicate this book to our parents, Jim and Lucy Shook, who brought us to Kanab in 1956. Congress funded the Glen Canyon Dam in April of that year, and in May, our dad arrived, brought down from Alaska by Project Construction Engineer Lem Wylie to set up the Bureau of Reclamation infrastructure in Kanab. Bureau offices would be there until the new town of Page, Arizona could be built. We went to high school both in Kanab and Fredonia, and in those short two years formed a lifelong attachment to the area

LIZ'S ACKNOWLEDGMENTS

Thanks to my critique group, Ann Acton, Terry Deighton, Tanya Parker Mills and Bonnie Harris for their weekly input as I began writing *Amy's Star*. To my beta readers, keen-eyed and quick, I appreciate your willingness to read and respond. Betas are: Joan Kirby, Nayna Christensen, Cheryl Brown, Terry Schnepf, Linda Chatterley, Sue Rasmussen, and Keralee Oblad. Also, thank you, Richard Madril, Bruce Raper, and Leon Christensen, for answering logistical or procedural questions I had as I was writing this. And, to my brother, Ron, thanks for the cover picture and for joining me in this endeavor.

Contents

Liz Adair & Ron Shook

AMY'S STAR
A SPIDER LATHAM CHRISTMAS STORY

by

LIZ ADAIR

Chapter One

SPIDER LATHAM GAZED at the green fiberglass box that had just been deposited at the edge of his back patio. A plastic poinsettia wreath hung on the door. "I don't think I've ever seen a porta-potty decorated for Christmas," he said.

"My wife done that." The driver folded up the lift gate. "She said anyone having sewer problems the day before Christmas needed something a little extra."

"Tell her thanks for the thought."

"No problem." The driver took off one work glove and offered his hand. "Bert Cummins."

"Spider Latham." Spider shook his hand.

"Say again?"

"Spider Latham."

"Like?" The driver made his hand look like a spider.

Spider nodded. How many times had he seen people do that? Must be the universal sign for *arachnid*. "It's a nickname." He looked around the back yard. "You ever been up here before?"

"Yeah. I serviced the site when ol' Jack was building this house. We went to school together, Jack Houghton and me."

"Oh?"

"Yeah. I thought he was crazy when he told me he was building a straw bale house. More like a straw bale

1

mansion." Bert pulled his glove on. "That was really something, him dying so quick like that and leaving everything to you."

The midmorning sun was well above the red cliffs behind his house, and Spider adjusted the brim of his Stetson. "Do you know where the septic tank is?"

Bert, on his way back to his truck, looked around and shrugged. "They put down all these pavers after the bathrooms was in, and it all looks different. He must have a half acre in concrete."

"Well, I'll run down to the courthouse and get the plans. They should be on file."

Bert swung up into the cab. "Don't bank on it. Jack tore down the old home place when he built. I'll bet he kept the old system."

Spider grimaced. He took two steps and touched the brim of his hat. "I'd better get a move-on then."

"Yeah. People generally close early on Christmas Eve." Bert shut his door and started his engine.

Spider turned and strode toward his pickup, his three-legged dog, Trey, at his heels. Detouring by the open kitchen window, he tapped on the edge of the screen. Smells of cinnamon and allspice wafted out along with holiday carols from the radio. "I'm going to town," he called. "See if I can get some information on locating the septic tank."

Spider's wife, Laurie, came over to the window, her auburn ponytail bobbing as she leaned over the counter to talk. She wore a red and green apron and had a smudge of flour on her cheek. "I'm sorry this happened just before Christmas. If you can't get it fixed today, we can get by."

"I'll get it taken care of." As Spider headed toward his pickup, he chewed on the last bit of information Bert had given him. No septic plan? Great suffering zot.

CB

Leaving the Planning Department empty handed, Spider almost ran into Toby Flint, a deputy he'd helped on the Red Pueblo problem last August.

"Spider!" Toby's face brightened. "I was just going out to your place."

"Delivering Christmas fruitcake?"

Toby blinked. "No. I hate fruitcake. I wanted to ask a favor."

Spider took a moment to survey the deputy. As always, his pants were creased and the leather on his black duty belt gleamed. "What is it?"

"Well, it's not exactly a favor. It's just that it's Christmas Eve and all."

Spider folded his arms and waited for Toby to get to the point.

Toby's face looked a little less hopeful. "I knew you had taken over Dr. Houghton's wounded birds."

"Wounded birds?"

"Yeah, you know. Amy and the rest of his charity cases."

Spider looked at the deputy searchingly. "You need help, Toby?"

Toby's eyes widened. "What? Me?" He laughed. "No. I'm fine." He looked up and down the hall and then pulled Spider away from the Planning Department door. "It's just that I found this young couple."

Spider frowned as he tried to follow Toby's narrative. "And?"

"He had a pry bar and was hanging around the newspaper stand. Mind you, he hadn't committed any crime."

"No," Spider agreed. "That doesn't sound criminal."

"Thing is, they don't have any money, and their car ran out of gas about a mile out of town."

"So, you think they're a couple of wounded birds?"

"They look pretty wounded to me. She looks to be about seventeen, and he's not too much older. They won't say where they're from."

Spider looked at his watch. He was no closer to an answer to his own dilemma, and Toby was trying to complicate his day.

"I gave them some toast," Toby said.

"What do you want me to do?" Impatience put an edge to Spider's voice, and Toby's cheeks began to redden.

"I thought maybe they could stay with you until we were able to locate their family."

"Why don't they stay with you?"

"I'm going up to see my girlfriend. I'm leaving this afternoon."

"What are you doing to locate the family? Are you sure they're as young as you say?"

"I'm tracing the car. As far as being sure, well, no. But wait 'til you see them." Toby was backing away. He must have sensed Spider's softening. "I'll bring them by on my way out of town. You'll see what I mean."

"You haven't yet *said* what you mean." Spider spoke to Toby's back, though. He was already halfway down the hall.

"Huh," Spider grunted, watching the deputy's well-shined heels go out the door.

He immediately dismissed Toby and his wounded birds and returned to the problem at hand. Next stop had to be Ace Hardware.

Chapter Two

ENTERING THE HARDWARE store, Spider set a course for the plumbing department. A clerk, name tag of Hank, met him at a stack of black pipe. "Anything I can do for you?"

"I'm looking for a probe. I've got to find a septic tank."

"How deep is it buried?"

"I haven't a clue."

"Where's it located?"

"It's Jack Houghton's place. You familiar with it?"

Hank shook his head. "Don't know that I am. We don't have any probes here at the store, but I've got one at home I'll loan you."

Spider looked at his watch. How long would he have to cool his heels waiting for Hank to get off?

Hank fished a set of keys out of his pocket. "My truck is in the lot. C'mon, and we'll run over and get it."

Spider followed him out through the back door and over to a yellow '83 Chevy pickup. Hank got in and leaned over to unlock the passenger door.

Spider climbed in and smelled the familiar old-pickup smell of oil and dust. "I appreciate this."

"Glad to do it." Hank started the engine, jockeyed around a forklift with a load of bricks, and pulled onto a city street heading north. "In fact, it's lucky for me."

"Oh?" Spider shifted in his seat. "How's that?"

"Well, I know you inherited Dr. Houghton's place."

"Yeah?"

"And along with that, you inherited Amy."

"Yeah. That too."

"Well . . ." Hank pulled into a driveway and braked to a stop, but he didn't finish his thought.

"You were saying," Spider prompted.

Hank cleared his throat. "Well, it may be nothing."

"But?"

"But she came in this morning and bought me out of Christmas lights."

"Christmas lights? When was this?"

"About a half hour before you came in."

Spider rubbed his jaw. "I wonder why she did that."

"She said something about the Bethlehem star." Hank left the motor running and opened his door. "Let me go get that probe, and I'll tell you about the rest of it on the way back."

Hank punched a button on the visor, got out, and ducked under the slowly rising garage door. Moments later he reappeared carrying a steel rod with a T-handle on top that he tossed in the bed, and then he got in the truck.

Spider watched him press the button to lower the door. "What's this about the Bethlehem star?"

Hank looked over his shoulder as he backed out. "I don't know. But she was grinning from ear to ear and told me she had been called to recreate the star right here in Kanab."

Spider's brows drew together. "She said *called?* Like it was a church assignment?"

Hank took off his baseball cap and put it on the dash. He hunched a shoulder and glanced at Spider. "I don't like saying this, but I thought you ought to know."

"Saying what? Know what? You haven't told me much yet."

"Well, the thing is, I know Amy's being treated for . . . that she's—"

"Bipolar," Spider said. Why did he feel so defensive? Amy wasn't his child. He hadn't even known her before last August.

"Yeah," Hank said. "The thing is, I remember how Amy was the day before she tried to ride in the Western Legends parade as Lady Godiva. She came into the store and bought a grundle of flat washers and some gold paint. She said she was fixin' to wire them together and make a kind of chain mail for her horse." Hank braked at an intersection and checked for traffic. "It turned out great, by the way. "

"If anyone had looked at it. I imagine all eyes were on her."

The corners of Hank's lips lifted. "Yep. She was quite a sight."

It irked Spider that the smile lingered for a full city block. "You were saying you remember how she was when she came in to get the washers."

"Oh. Right. Well, like I was saying, when she came in to get the washers, she was like she was this morning. Big grin. Spilling over with information about what she was going to do. Talking a mile a minute. If you don't mind my saying so, she seemed a bit manic."

Spider sighed. "I suppose everyone in town knows about her illness."

Hank seemed to think it over and then nodded. "You know that saying—it takes a village to raise a child? Well, it takes a village to watch out for Amy, too."

"Sounds more like the village was staring at her."

Hank shook his head decisively. "I was at the staging area for the parade, and as soon as she rode up, somebody grabbed the raffle quilt and wrapped it around her."

"Did she ride in the parade?"

"Nah. Someone called Dr. Houghton, and he came and got her." Hank turned into the lumberyard and parked his pickup. "But today was like that. Made me wonder if she might need to see her doctor."

Spider's jaw tightened. It seemed like everyone was a diagnostician. "I'll check it out, but tell me again what she said about the star."

Hank turned off the key and grabbed his hat off the dash. "I told you all I know. She said she had been called to recreate the Bethlehem star."

"Here in Kanab?"

"Yes. Here in Kanab." Hank got out.

Spider got out, too, and stood on the other side of the pickup bed. "But she didn't say *who* had called her?"

Hank, hat still in his hand, scratched his head and then raised his eyes to meet Spider's. "Holy cow."

"What do you mean, holy cow?"

"I thought she was talking about something else."

Spider reached in and got the probe, hefting it like he would a spear. "Spit it out, man. Tell me what she said."

Hank took the time to put on his hat. His eyes went from the long metal rod in Spider's hand to his face and back. "She said it was President Obama."

Spider spoke under his breath. "Great suffering zot." He took off for the parking lot, pausing to look back at Hank and lift the tool. "Thanks for this. I'll bring it back after Christmas."

"No problem."

Spider strode to his pickup and dropped the probe in the back. As he got in, he pulled his cell phone out of his pocket and brought up Laurie's number.

Christmas music in the background told him she had answered before he heard her greeting.

"Hello, Darlin'," he said. "Has Amy come home yet?"

"No. I haven't seen her. She called a while ago from Crosby's Hardware asking how long your heavy duty extension cord was."

"Not Ace Hardware?"

"No. I'm sure she said Crosby's. Why?"

"I think we've got a problem. This one may be bigger than the drains."

Chapter Three

WHEN SPIDER GOT home, he saw that Amy's pickup was in the driveway with cardboard boxes stacked high above the sides of the bed. Trey came to meet him, and he leaned down to pat her head. "Where's Amy, Trey dog? Let's see if she's in the kitchen."

At the back door, he could see Laurie at the table with Amy opposite. They both looked up as Spider opened the door.

"Hi," Laurie said. She smiled, but it wasn't an automatic, come-from-the-heart, Christmas Eve smile. It was a wooden, brave-faced turning up of her lips.

Amy smiled, too. Hers was genuine. Five-hundred-watt incandescent.

"Hello, girls," Spider said. "How's it going?"

"Fantastic," Amy said. "Did you see my truck?"

"Caught a glimpse of it." He turned one of the chairs around and straddled it, putting his Stetson on the table. "Is that my Christmas present?"

Amy laughed. "Your present has been under the tree for a week. I know you know because I saw you shaking it the other day."

Laurie broke in. "Amy stopped taking her meds."

"So I heard." Spider tipped his head, regarding Amy. "Is that wise?"

Amy covered her face. "No. I know it's not, but listen." She let her hands slide down, so her eyes were peeking above her fingertips. "I just wanted to feel the Christmas joy. You don't know what it's like to have everything—" She made a horizontal motion. "—even out. I want to *feel something* this Christmas!"

Spider grimaced. He understood what Amy was saying, and right now he hated the responsibility he had inherited. "This thing with President Obama and the Bethlehem star. It wasn't real, you know."

Amy stared at Spider, chewing on her lower lip. "The big black limo? The tinted windows going silently down?" She pantomimed the windows lowering. "The man in the back leaning forward and taking my hand, telling me he had this great thing for me to do? You're saying it wasn't real?"

Spider nodded. "That's what I'm saying."

Amy looked at Laurie. "It was real to me."

The stove buzzer sounded, and Laurie jumped up and grabbed a hot pad. As she opened the oven, she spoke over her shoulder. "What about after Christmas? What then?"

Amy raised her hand like she was testifying. "Day after tomorrow. Back on my meds. I promise."

Spider pointed. "That's your left hand."

Amy's grin grew in size. "That means the promise goes double."

Spider stood. "It better."

Amy stood, too. "Besides, I've got so much to do before tonight, I need all this energy."

Spider put the chair back and picked up his hat. "Bethlehem star, huh?"

"It's gonna be spectacular!" Amy hugged Laurie, catching her with a cookie midway from the pan to the cooling rack. "Oops. Five second rule. I'll eat that one." She bent down to pick up the snickerdoodle that had fallen to the floor.

Spider set his Stetson on his head, still speaking to Amy. "Did Laurie tell you about the drain situation?"

Amy nodded and answered with her mouth full. "Go potty in the privy outside. Shower standing in a washtub. All water gets thrown on the flowerbeds. I got it."

Spider picked up one of the cool cookies and regarded Amy. She was short and square, and her straight blonde hair hung in a pixie cut over her blue eyes.

"How long did you live here with Jack?" he asked. "Do you know where the septic tank is?"

Amy shook her head. "I'd help you look, but I've got to find a place to put my star. Want to help me for a minute?"

Spider looked at his watch. The morning was just about gone. In a couple hours, any parts he might need to fix the drains would be out of reach as stores closed for Christmas.

"Spider?" Laurie came over to him and spoke softly. "This Christmas needs to last her a lifetime."

"Unless she makes the holiday med vacation an annual affair," he murmured. "But okay." He held up his hands. "If you don't mind freezing your buns off tonight going out to the privy, I'm fine with that."

Laurie grinned. "I'll warm them up on you when I come back in."

Spider pulled her to him. "I'm fine with that, too." He planted a kiss on her mouth.

Amy spoke from the back door. "Pul-eeze. You've got a tender young thing listening to this. I'm blushing."

Spider snorted, but he refrained from any comments about Lady Godiva as he followed Amy out.

Spider left his jacket on the peg by the door. It was a shirtsleeve-weather day, and the sun took any edge off the preceding night's December chill as it climbed toward noon. "What do you need me to do?" he asked as they crossed the expanse of pavers.

She stopped at the edge and pointed to the red bluff that began rising about a hundred yards in back of the barn. "See the tree at the top?"

"You planning on putting your star on top of that tree?"

Amy shook her head. "I want to anchor one end of a line on that tree and the other end down here somewhere. I need you to help me do that."

"You're going to have a heck of a lot of line," Spider said. "Stores close in a couple of hours."

"I got a thousand feet of poly rope. That's all Crosby's had."

"That'll do." Spider traced the trajectory from the cliff down to the base of the barn. "Let's go have a look-see, figure what we can hook onto."

They found an eyebolt in the barn foundation, and fifteen minutes later, Amy was jogging up a trail with a ball of parachute cord in her hand.

"Call me when you get to the top," Spider shouted after her.

She waved to show she heard him and continued her ascent.

He stood watching for a moment and then went to his pickup to get the probe. Returning to the back yard with Trey at his heels, he surveyed the area. The pavers were laid out in a random pattern that created an attractive, low maintenance, low water landscape. But where was the septic access?

He crossed to the open kitchen window and tapped on the frame. "Laurie, can you come out for a minute?"

The back door opened. "What d'ya need?" she asked.

"You came to visit Jack when he was young. Do you know where the old house was located?"

She stepped out onto the patio and walked from the covered area into the sunshine. Shading her eyes, she looked around. "Everything's different, but I think the old home place was in this same spot. I think Jack tore it down and built his house in the same place."

"Huh."

"What's that?"

"I just said huh."

"No. It sounds like a truck coming up the driveway." Laurie walked over to look through the breezeway between the house and the garage. "It's a tow truck," she called back to Spider. "And Toby's right behind."

"Aw, shoot. Toby's wounded birds." Spider strode over to Laurie and stood, hands on hips, as Deputy Flint got out of his pickup.

"Toby's bringing us some birds?"

Spider didn't answer Laurie but called to the deputy, "I thought you were coming after lunch."

"I was, but I need to get up the road. I figured a couple hours sooner wasn't going to change anything drastically." Toby beckoned. "Come and meet Grace and Ben."

Spider waved to Vic, the tow truck driver who had gotten out and was busy unloading a tired looking Honda Civic. When Spider turned back to greet his Christmas guests, he silently agreed with Toby's assessment. Neither one looked over seventeen.

The young man was of average height but thin and pale. The girl, waif-like, had dark eyes too big for her face. She pulled her shapeless cardigan around her, but it couldn't disguise the size and shape of her belly. It looked like she was hiding a basketball under her tee shirt.

Spider's heart sank. A wounded bird for sure—one that looked like it was about ready to lay an egg.

Chapter Four

LAURIE SWEPT BY Spider and put an arm around each of the young people. "We're so glad to have you," she said. "Are you staying for Christmas? That will be nice."

Neither of the visitors said a word, but as they walked through the breezeway with Laurie, the waif bent down to rub Trey behind the ears.

Spider turned to Toby. "What have you found out? Who are they?"

"I know their first names. Grace and Ben."

"You said that. What else? Didn't he have a driver's license? Car registration?"

Toby turned up his hands. "What do you want me to say? They don't have them. They don't want to say who they are."

"You're tracing the car?"

"Yeah, but it's Christmas Eve." Toby looked at his watch. "I gotta get going." He patted his pocket. "It's gonna be a special Christmas in Panguitch."

"Oh?"

Toby waved at the departing tow truck. "Yes, sir. I'm gonna pop the old question-a-roonie."

Spider smiled. "Is that right? Well, you'd better get on the road."

Toby twisted his hands together. "You got any words of advice, Spider?"

"Me? Why would you want advice from me?"

"Well, you know. You and Laurie. You've got a good thing going. How'd you ask her?"

Spider laughed. "She asked me. I was beating around the bush, making a hash of it. Ring in my pocket, just like you. Finally, she said, 'You want to get married?' I said yep, and there you go."

Toby kicked a rock off the driveway. "I don't know if that makes me feel better or not."

"Nothing will make you feel better until you give it a go. Now, on your way. I'll take care of those two young 'uns until you find out where they belong."

"You're right. I've just got to do it." Toby sketched a salute and turned to his pickup. As he got in the cab, he called, "Merry Christmas."

"Merry Christmas. Call me as soon as you know anything." Spider waved and turned to walk back through the breezeway to the back yard. He paused there, wanting to get started on finding the septic tank but knowing he should go in and make conversation with their guests.

He looked up at the cliff with its red rocks sharply outlined against the cobalt sky and searched for Amy. There she was halfway up. He'd pop into the house for a minute. Amy's shout would be a good excuse to leave.

As he opened the back door, he breathed in the heavy fragrance of onions and celery floating on vaporized molecules of chicken fat. Spying Grace and Ben single-mindedly consuming bowls of soup, Spider asked, "Is it lunchtime already?"

"Not yet. They haven't had a meal since yesterday morning, so I gave them some soup to hold them over until noon. I intended to make rolls, but today hasn't turned out the way I planned."

Grace paused with her spoon halfway to her mouth and turned her dark, sad eyes on Laurie.

"Oh, not you, dear." Laurie moved over to squeeze her shoulders. "I meant the drain thing."

Ben showed the most life since they had pulled in. He sat up and looked from Laurie to Spider and back. "What about the drains?"

Spider answered. "They're plugged."

"Did you try a snake?"

Spider gritted his teeth, counted to five, and tried to remove the edge from his reply. "Yeah."

Ben finished his soup in three hasty bites and stood. "Where's your septic tank?"

Laurie must have seen that Spider didn't have the patience to answer questions from someone who looked like he hadn't yet begun shaving. She answered. "We're not sure where it is."

Spider opened the door. "I'm going out to see if I can find it."

"I'll come help," Ben said. "You got a probe?"

Without answering, Spider went out, walked to the middle of the patio, and looked up at the bluff behind the barn. He could see Amy, a toy soldier in a white blouse, scrambling to the top.

"What're you looking at?" Ben asked.

Spider pointed. "Amy. She just made it to the top. C'mon."

Ben walked beside Spider as he strode to the barn. "We're going up there?"

"Nah. She's going to throw a line down and pull up a rope."

"What for?"

"She's going to hang a Bethlehem star as high as she can. She's going to hook the rope to that tree that sits on the edge."

"Cool."

Spider walked to the back of the barn where a crowbar leaned against the wall. Amy's spool of poly rope sat by it.

"So, how's she planning on getting her star up there?" Ben asked, still tagging along.

"I haven't asked her."

"If you put a loop in the rope out about fifty feet, that'd give you enough to go around the tree and go over the bank. If you had a pulley, you could hang it on that loop, and you'd have an easy way to get the star up." Ben looked up at the tree again. "How high you figure that is?"

"Probably three hundred feet. Maybe more."

"You got a pulley?"

Spider regarded the young man. He didn't look like much. His face was thin, and his eyes were a washed-out blue with light-colored eyelashes, but he had shed his jacket in the mildness of the day, and his arms looked like he was used to physical work. "You know how to tie a bowline?" Spider asked.

"Sure."

"I'm not sure Amy does. Do you want to hike up there and help, if she needs it? Don't let her tie a granny."

Ben glanced around. "Where's the trail?"

Spider pointed. "Behind the garden plot. It snakes up from there."

Ben nodded and started off at a trot.

"Good idea about the pulley," Spider called after him.

He raised a hand in acknowledgement as he continued up the trail.

Spider went to his newly built shop on the other side of the barn. He and Laurie had gone round and round about what the shop would look like. Spider had said they couldn't afford anything but a metal clad pole building, but Laurie was adamant that the shop should match the Pueblo-type architecture of house and barn.

"We've got the money. We can afford it," she had said.

"It's Jack's money," Spider had countered.

"It's yours now. The shop matches."

She got the last word, and Spider had to admit she'd been right. He entered the shop and quickly found the pulley he needed. He grabbed another large coil of parachute cord and stuffed it under his arm. Standing a moment beside the workbench, he mentally walked through the process of hooking the rope to the eyebolt. He decided he needed a come-along to cinch it tight and lifted one down from the pegboard wall. Then he returned to the area behind the barn where they were going to tether the star.

He pulled out fifty feet of Amy's rope and, heeding Ben's suggestion, tied a loop and attached the pulley. He had just finished when his phone rang. He searched three pockets before he found it. "Yeah?"

Amy was on the other end. "Ben tossed down the line. We're ready to haul up the rope."

"Okay. Give me a minute to get to the bottom of the cliff."

"We can see you."

Spider looked up, and when Amy waved, he waved the pulley in reply. "Anything else?"

"Just that I can tie a bowline. But thanks for sending Ben up. His arm is better for throwing the line down."

"No problem." Spider punched the off button then grabbed the pry bar leaning against the barn and put it through the hole in the rope reel. He hung the bundle of parachute cord on it, too, and picked up the pulley.

It was an awkward load, but he managed to call Laurie while he walked towards the bluff. When she answered, he asked her to come out and help for a minute.

By the time he reached the red, rocky scree at the bottom of the bluff, Laurie had trotted out to join him. Grace followed with the dog beside her.

"It's a ways out here," Laurie said, puffing a bit. "What d'ya need?"

Spider had dropped his burdens and had his hands on his hips, scanning the area. "We need to find the line Amy and Ben threw down from the top."

Laurie's auburn pony tail hung halfway down her back as she shaded her eyes and craned her neck. "Are they up there?"

"Yeah. They're back from the edge, though. You won't be able to see them."

Grace joined them. "Is that what you're looking for?"

Spider searched the area she was pointing to and finally saw the white cord hanging down. "That's it," he called. He strode to where the cord lay on the ground. He had tied a heavy bolt on the end for ballast, and he removed that now, dropped it in his pocket, and tied the cord through a loop he had put in the end of the poly rope.

"What do you need me to do?" Laurie asked.

"You see the pulley?" Spider tossed her the bundle of cord.

She picked up the parachute line. "Wow? Do you think you have enough of this?"

"It's got to reach to the top and back down," Spider said. "I need you to thread it through the pulley and let it unwind. Keep track of both ends as Amy pulls the rope up."

"I can help you," Grace said. "You hold the pulley, and I'll put the cord through."

Spider started walking toward the barn. "I'm going to unroll the rope and get ready to tie it off to the barn as soon as she gets it up there." The reel spun on the pry-bar axle leaving a line of rope in the dirt. When he got halfway there, Amy called on her phone.

"Can I start hauling up?"

Spider glanced at Laurie and Grace. They looked ready.

"Haul away," he said. "When you get it tied off to the tree, come on down and we'll have lunch."

It took them almost an hour to get the rope up and anchored from the tree to the barn. The pulley hung about ten feet below the top of the bluff, the double length of parachute cord trailing to the bottom. They were ready to hoist up the Bethlehem star.

Amy shouted down from the top. "Wow-ee! It's gonna be spectacular!"

Chapter Five

SPIDER BLEW ON his spoonful of soup to cool it. "So," he said in a conversational tone. "We haven't had a chance to get through the usual small talk with Ben and Grace. Might as well do that right now."

"Oh, I don't know," Laurie said, her eyes twinkling. "Grace and I did some small talking."

Grace looked down at her soup. "Very small, I'm afraid."

Laurie patted her hand. "Don't worry, dear. We don't need a lot of information. We're just glad you're with us for Christmas."

Amy looked around the table. "What's going on?"

Laurie smiled. "Grace and Ben were on their way south, but they ran out of gas. Their resources are slender at the moment."

"Jack used to call it embarrassed circumstances." Amy chuckled. "He brought so many people home in that condition that we started shortening it to EC." Leaning her chin on her fist, she asked Grace, "Where were you going?"

Ben's and Grace's eyes met, and he answered the question. "We'd rather not say."

Amy shrugged. "Suit yourself." She turned to Laurie. "How's Goldie doing?"

Laurie grimaced. "I think she's getting close. I checked her this morning, and all the signs point to tomorrow or the next day." She turned to Ben and Grace to explain. "We're keeping a horse for a friend who is away for several years."

"She's in the slammer," Amy added.

Laurie put her hand on Amy's knee and went on with her explanation. "I didn't realize that the mare was pregnant, but when I talked to Dorrie, the owner, she said that last winter a wild stallion jumped the fence and was in Goldie's pasture. Dorrie didn't know she had been bred."

"And she wasn't supposed to let her have any babies," Spider said. "Goldie has a deformed hoof that's hereditary. She could pass it on to her foal."

Grace looked at Spider with her large, waif eyes. "That's terrible."

"Well, it's done now. We'll just see what happens." Laurie pushed the soup pot toward her guests. "Have some more."

Grace put up her hands. "I couldn't eat another bite. Thank you. It was so good."

"Both times," Ben said.

Laurie stood and began gathering dishes. "Save room for turkey and trimmings this evening."

Grace stood too, her hand on her back. "Can I help you with dinner?"

"Sure." Laurie's brows came together as she looked up from the pile of crockery. "Is something wrong?"

Grace rubbed a spot in her lumbar area. "I've got this pain that comes and goes. Must be from sleeping in the car last night."

Spider stood and pushed his chair in. "Well, you'll sleep well tonight. The east guest room has a king sized bed in it."

Neither Ben nor Grace said anything but both had a rosy flush climb up their cheeks. She looked at her feet. He looked at the back door as if seeking an escape route.

Ben slowly stood. "Um. We're not…" He pointed from himself to Grace. "We're not married or anything like that."

In the silence that followed Ben's remark, Spider studiously avoided looking at Grace's pregnant belly. Laurie resumed stacking soup bowls, and Spider joined her, glad for something to occupy his attention.

Amy was the one who finally spoke. "Who's going to help me with the Bethlehem star?"

Ben and Grace spoke together. "I will."

Grace looked at Laurie. "Unless you need me right now to help with dinner."

"No," Laurie said. "You go on. If you'll come in about four, that'll be plenty of time."

Spider paused on his way to the sink with his hands full of dishes. "I'd better see if I can find the septic tank, Amy. Call me if you need me, though."

"I will," she promised. Then she clattered out the door with Grace right behind her.

The last in line, Ben paused with his hand on the knob. "Oh, by the way. I've got an idea where the tank might be."

"Oh?" Spider wiped his hands on a dishtowel.

Ben held the door open. "Come out, and I'll show you."

Spider took his hat off the hook by the door and followed Ben outside.

Pointing to where pavers were laid in a pinwheel pattern, Ben said, "I think this may be where it is. The pattern for the whole back yard starts here."

"Huh," Spider grunted. "You may be right."

"I saw it from up above. From down here it all looks pretty random."

Spider's eyes traced the lines as they spiraled out from the few tiles under his feet. Funny he had never noticed the pattern that spread out from here, halfway between the back door and the breezeway.

"Only one way to find out if it's under here," Spider said. "They're sand-set pavers. Come up easy."

"Want help?"

Spider's attention was captured by the laughter of Amy and Grace coming through the breezeway, each on an end of a roll of chicken wire with Trey following close behind. "Should Grace be carrying that? Maybe you'd better go help them."

"Omygosh!" Ben took off at a trot, calling, "Grace, let me take that for you."

Spider paused to watch him take the wire roll, hoist it on his shoulder, and follow Amy toward the back of the barn. Grace brought up the rear, resting at the corner of the barn, leaning her shoulder against the wall with her hand on the small of her back. Better keep an eye on that.

Then he headed through the breezeway to get the tools he needed to test out Ben's theory about what lay under the paver pinwheel.

Chapter Six

WHILE THE YOUNG folks worked on Amy's star, Spider found the septic tank, right where Ben thought it would be. He called Burt Cummins and made arrangements for him to come and pump it out first thing the day after Christmas.

Satisfied with that small accomplishment, he put his tools away and came into the shop to finish Laurie's Christmas present. He had made a branding iron for her with her *Double L* brand and still needed to paint the wooden handle.

He took a small can of enamel off a shelf and began to shake it. Laurie liked red. Still shaking with the can with one hand, he chose a paintbrush and set it on the bench. The door opened behind him, and he sprang in front of the bench, spreading his arms to hide the gift.

Ben peeked through the door. "Okay if I come in?"

Spider exhaled. "You scared me."

Ben remained with just his shoulder in the door.

"Come on in," Spider invited. "I'm finishing up something I made for Laurie."

Ben approached the workbench. "That's an interesting Christmas present."

"She's been wanting one." Spider brushed a wood shaving off the bench. "By the way, I didn't tell you thanks for pointing me in the right direction to find that tank."

"Glad to help." Ben put his hands in his pockets and looked around. "This is quite a shop."

"It's a work in progress." Spider leaned against the workbench. "Everything going all right in the Bethlehem star department?"

Ben folded his arms and rested his weight on the bench, too. "That Amy is a gal with a plan. Did you know she bought ten thousand lights?"

"Ten thousand!"

Ben smiled. "I talked her out of using all of them. They're LED, so they don't draw what regular lights do, but I don't think she realized that she can't string out that much extension cord without losing significant power."

"Oh, shoot!" Spider grimaced. "I've been so uptight about the drain situation that I didn't even think of that."

Ben stood and looked around again. "You got a generator?"

"Yeah. What're you thinking?"

"I figured if we put it right below the star, then we'd only have to run cord from the generator up to where it's hanging. We could manage that."

"The generator's in the storeroom. Let's go get it."

Spider led the way through a wide door into a room full of large tools and equipment laid out on industrial shelving. The generator sat underneath the shelves on the floor, and Spider pointed to it.

Ben pulled it out and stood up, hands on hips. "Grace's pregnant," he said.

"Beg pardon?"

Ben ran his hand through his hair. "You took us in. Fed us. I don't feel good about keeping things secret, even though Grace wants me to."

Spider stifled a smile. "I hate to tell you this, Ben, but Grace being pregnant is no secret."

Ben made an impatient gesture. "I know that, but I meant the story behind it all."

Spider pulled a stack of empty five gallon buckets from the shelf beside him. He pulled off two, handing one to Ben and turning the other over on the concrete floor. "Have a seat, son, and tell me your story. Start from the beginning."

Ben sat on his makeshift stool and leaned back, propping himself against the shelving brace. "The beginning." He screwed up his face in thought. "I would say the beginning was my junior year."

"High school? Where was that?"

"Salt Lake City. I had been placed with a new foster family, and that meant a new school. Grace and I had fifth period choir together."

"You're smiling," Spider observed. "Must be a nice memory."

"It is. I fell in love with her on that first day."

"And she? Did she reciprocate?"

"It took a year to win her, but by Christmas of our senior year—last Christmas—she told me she loved me." Ben sighed. "But . . ."

"Let me guess," Spider said. "Her family didn't want her getting serious so early."

"There's just her and her mom. But I think it was more than her getting serious so young."

"What was it, then?"

Ben shrugged. "I didn't have the proper background. Or aspirations."

Spider's brows went up. "How so?"

"Well, first there was the foster child thing. Maybe that would have been overlooked if I had earned a scholarship to a prestigious school."

"No scholarship, huh?"

Ben smiled and looked down at his shoes. "Oh I got a scholarship."

"Must have been to a state college."

Ben shook his head. "Worse. It was to a tech school in Phoenix that was coupled with an electrician apprenticeship." He looked up at Spider, his eyes sparkling. "It's a great program. I can support myself while I go to school. And when I finish, I'll have a good paying job."

"And you have a natural aptitude."

Ben paused, as if struck by what Spider had said. "You know, I do have an aptitude. I'm top of my class."

Spider folded his arms and stretched his long legs out in front of him. "But Grace's mama wasn't going to have her tying herself to someone who worked with his hands."

Ben's brows came down, and his mouth formed a grim line. "You got that right. When spring break rolled around, Mrs. Engle set Grace up with the son of her boss. He was a college man. Princeton."

"I suppose he had the right background and aspirations."

Ben picked up a bolt lying on the shelf beside him and began unscrewing the nut from the end, his eyes on the task. "He might have had the right aspirations, but he had no morals and no compunction about drugging and raping a young girl."

"Great suffering zot! Is that what happened?"

Ben nodded, still intent on the piece of metal in his hands.

"What did Grace's mother say?"

"Grace never told her."

Spider whistled under his breath. "So the mother doesn't know? How could that happen?"

Ben finally looked up. "Grace's mother is a career woman, a producer for a TV station in Salt Lake. Very successful. Very busy. She loves Grace, but her way of showing it always has to do with things that will bring prestige."

"Like getting her a date with a Princeton man?"

Ben nodded. "Or sending her to an expensive school."

"Where is this school?"

"It's a performing arts college in Seattle. Grace left Salt Lake in mid-August."

"And she didn't come home for Thanksgiving?"

When Ben shook his head in reply, Spider counted on his fingers. "So she'd have been five months along when she left?"

"About four and a half, the best I can figure." Ben's cheeks got red. "I don't know much about it, but I've done some reading online since she told me."

"And she told you when?"

"What's today? Wednesday? She called me Saturday. Her mother had sent her the plane tickets home, and she didn't know what to do. I was the first one she'd told."

"This last Saturday?" Spider pulled his legs in and sat forward, frowning. "Great suffering zot! Did she think if she ignored the situation, it would go away?"

Ben laid the bolt back on the shelf beside him and looked Spider in the eye. "I won't let you be angry with her. She's gone through a hellish four months in a strange place with no friends and no one to help her." Ben dropped his eyes. "I should have been there for her, but when she quit emailing or calling, I figured it was because she had finally listened to her mother."

Spider patted Ben's knee. "I'm not angry with her, but why'd she quit writing?"

"She thought—" Ben's voice broke, and he had to try again. "She thought I wouldn't love her anymore because of what happened." He paused and cleared his throat. "Anyway, she called me, and I said I'd pick her up and take her home with me. She changed her tickets, but because of the holiday, the nearest flight she could find was to Las Vegas." He spread his hands. "I had enough money for gas both ways, but then my starter went out."

"And there went your gas money," Spider said. "I understand. But, if you were going to Phoenix, why come this way? It's closer from Las Vegas to go by Kingman."

"One of my instructors got me a day's work at the trading post at Cameron. My plan was to work there today, and we could be home by Christmas."

"So what're you going to do when you get to Phoenix?"

"Get married. I've got a small apartment. It's a studio, but there'll be room for the baby, too. We'll manage."

Spider rubbed his jaw. "That sounds okay, but what about her mother? If Grace didn't arrive at the airport on her scheduled flight, wouldn't her mom do something? Like call out the police?"

Ben shook his head. "Her flight was scheduled for today, and Mrs. Engle is working tonight. She does it every year, so more of the crew can be off. Grace was supposed to take a cab home and see her mom in the morning."

Spider stood and picked up his bucket. "Okay. But if you're going to marry Grace, you need to start off right. Be square with her mom. If Grace won't call her mother, you need to do it. Let her know her daughter is safe and that you intend to take care of her—and the baby—from now on."

Ben smacked his palm down on one of the steel shelves and spoke through clenched teeth. "I just know she's going to think I did this to Grace."

"She may at first, but that's not important. What's important is your relationship with Grace. Mrs. Engle will soon see that her daughter made the right choice."

Ben rose and gave his bucket to Spider. "You're right. If I get crossways with her mom, it will only distress Grace."

Spider put the stack back on the shelf and looked at his watch. "You'd better get that generator out there and get it hooked up before dark. Haul it in the back of the old pickup, the one with the dented roof. He pulled a key ring from his pocket, showed Ben the right key, and handed it over. "Just leave the truck there for tonight."

Ben pocketed the keys and rolled the generator to the storeroom door. He got it over the threshold and halfway to the shop entrance before he stopped. "You should see the star that Amy designed," he said. "Want to come help?"

Spider went to his workbench and picked up the can of red paint. "I need to get this done. You go on."

"Okay." Ben opened the shop door. "But wait till you see it. It's going to be spectacular."

Chapter Seven

DINNER WAS A merry affair. The turkey, brown and succulent, looked like something out of a magazine. Ben declared Grace's mashed potatoes and Amy's bread stuffing amazing, and everyone agreed. They topped it off with pumpkin pie, and then all worked together to put the food away and get the dishes done. Amy washed them in a dishpan and carried the water outside after they were done and dumped it on the chrysanthemums.

"We're eating reruns tomorrow," Laurie announced.

"Suits me." Ben put a stack of plastic storage containers in the fridge.

Laurie paused with a dishcloth in her hand, looked at the clock, and then at Spider. "I think I need to go out to the stable. Can we do our Christmas Eve out there?"

"You think Goldie's that close?"

Grace's eyes grew huge. "Are you frightened?"

Laurie smiled at her. "No. I'm sure she can handle everything herself. Being there is more for me than for the mare."

"I'll put the Buddy heater in the tack room and grab two cots," Spider said.

"You're keeping me company?" Laurie kissed him on the cheek. "We'll need camp chairs, too." She finished wiping the counters and set the cloth by the sink. "Better get your jackets," she said to Amy and Grace. "And grab some blankets from the upstairs hall closet."

"I'll get them," Amy said, trotting through the living room to the broad staircase that swept up to the second floor. She stopped halfway and leaned against the wrought iron railing. "Spider, when we read the Christmas story, we need to have the star shining above us," she called. "It's dark out. Let's turn it on right now."

Spider laughed as he put on his Stetson. "Okay. As soon as we get everything out to the tack room, we'll all go out and watch as you plug it in."

Everyone helped carry blankets, and they trooped out through the back door.

"Brrr. It's chilly," Laurie said.

"Not bad for December." Spider looked around. "It's supposed to stay above freezing tonight."

"Are you rethinking whether you want to spend the night in the barn?" Amy asked.

"We'll be fine. The heater will keep it warm." Spider opened the tack room door, held it for everyone to enter, and followed the group inside. He dropped the quilts on a saddle. "C'mon, Ben. Let's get the rest of the gear."

Ben set his blankets on an adjacent rack and followed Spider outside. "Boy it's dark!" he said as Spider closed the door behind them.

"Not much of a moon." Spider pulled a flashlight out of his jacket pocket. "We'll have a crescent later, but it's not up yet."

Ben put his hands in his pocket and paused to look up at the black matte sky studded with twinkling points of light. "Amy's star should show up pretty good."

They reached the shop, and Spider opened the door and turned on the light. Back in the storeroom, they found everything they needed and retraced their steps to the shop door. Spider let Ben go outside first then balanced his load, so he could reach the light switch.

Before he could flip it down, the lights went out.

"Whoa!" Ben said. "Did you do that?"

"Do what?"

"Turn out all the lights?" Ben walked a few tentative steps. "Oh, wow."

"What?"

"Look toward Kanab. The whole countryside is dark."

"Huh." Spider juggled his burdens, so he could close the door and then get the flashlight out of his pocket. "Wonder what happened." He turned on the torch and they followed the circle of light to the stable and opened the door.

Laurie's voice sounded loud in the dark. "Spider? Did you flip a breaker?"

"Nope. The power's off all over."

"What do you mean by all over?" Grace's voice trembled, and Spider found her with the beam. Careful not to shine it in her face, he kept her illuminated until Ben could set the heater down and go to her.

Spider lowered the chairs and cots to the floor. "Amy, I'm going to ask you to wait a while longer for your star. I'll go get some more flashlights and a couple of lanterns. Hang tough. You won't be in the dark much longer."

As he stepped out the door, he heard an intake of breath and then Grace's tremulous voice. "Is he taking the light?"

"I'll be right back," Spider promised and set off toward the shop again.

Finding what he needed proved more difficult than he would have thought. With only the flashlight's slender beam to aid him, he finally found the lanterns hanging on the pegboard. He located spare batteries and the place on a high shelf where he had stashed four extra flashlights. With his arms full, he pulled the door closed and walked as quickly as he could to the stable.

When he opened the tack room door, he was greeted by Amy's cheer. "Now it's starlight time."

"Wait a minute," Spider said. "Everyone gets a flashlight."

Someone exhaled, and then Grace spoke, her voice stouter now. "Thank you."

Spider handed out lights, and when all were ready, he announced, "It is now time to turn on Amy's Bethlehem star."

Out of the tack room, they went around to the back of the barn and tramped across the field. Spider oriented himself by illuminated glimpses of the pickup that held the generator, sitting three hundred feet below Amy's chicken wire contraption. He looked up but could see nothing except the dark outline of the cliff blocking out the view of the spangled sky.

Spider heard somebody stumble and shined his light to see who it was. "Careful, Grace," he said.

"I've got her," Ben answered. "You guys go on. We're going to stop and rest a moment."

Spider paused, trying to see from Grace's countenance how she was doing. Her hand was on her back, and her mouth was compressed, but she looked toward Spider and smiled. "I'm fine," she said. "Just a stitch in my back."

"Okay," Spider said. "But call if it doesn't get better."

"It's better already," Grace said.

Spider turned his flashlight back to the ground in front of him and continued the trek to the pickup.

Laurie, walking beside him, said in a low voice, "I don't like the look of that back ache."

"You think Goldie isn't the only one that's getting close to time?" Spider looked back and saw the twin beams of Ben and Grace's flashlights bobbing as they walked. "If that's so, is it all right for her to be way out here?"

"She'll be fine. The walk is probably good for her."

Laurie glanced around and then added, "Though it would be a good idea to keep track of how often the stitch returns."

Spider glanced at his watch. "It's seven thirty."

"Good to know," Laurie murmured.

Ahead of them, Amy broke into a trot.

"She's going to break her neck," Spider said between his teeth.

Laurie chuckled. "She's excited."

They tracked Amy's progress by way of her flashlight's erratic movements as she reached the pickup and climbed into the bed. "Ready?" she called.

"Do you know how to start the generator?" Spider called back.

Amy bent over with her light shining down. "Is this the one that Jack had?"

Spider and Laurie were just about there, and he waited to answer until he could speak in a normal tone. "Yes. His is quieter than mine, and I thought that'd be better."

"Then I know how to start it." Amy handed him her torch. "Can you hold this?"

As Spider held the light, Laurie asked, "Where is the star?"

"It's above us but a bit closer to the cliff face," Spider said. "I don't think you'll have any problem seeing where it is."

Amy straightened up and announced, "Everyone except Spider turn off your lights."

All complied, and the darkness pressed around them, pushed back by the golden circle in back of the pickup. Amy's movements were crisp as she pushed two rocker switches and pulled on the starter rope. The generator sprang into life, and when it was running smoothly, she plugged in the line hanging down from above.

Spider turned off his flashlight and looked up, blinking as Amy's star burst forth. She had fashioned it into a glowing orb with a major axis of shimmering light sticking through like a knitting needle stuck into a ball of yarn. Six smaller rays fanned out at different angles. It looked like something an artist would put on a Christmas card, a beautiful, gleaming starburst hanging in a black velvet sky.

Nobody spoke. They all stood silently, heads back, mouths open, eyes fixed on Amy's stellar stand-in.

Spider's throat constricted, and he felt a warm glow in his chest. He wiped his right eye with the heel of his hand to clear his vision and swallowed to get rid of the lump in his throat. When he could finally speak, his words were hushed, as if he were standing in a sacred place. "You were right, Amy. It truly is spectacular."

Chapter Eight

WHEN THE NIGHT became too chilly, they finally moved back to the stable, but Amy wouldn't hear of going inside. "Ben, you get the chairs, and Spider, you get the heater and bring it out here. I'll get the blankets. We can wrap up and look at the star while we listen to the Christmas story."

Laurie stayed in the tack room to check on Goldie through a window into her adjacent stall, and the rest of them arranged the chairs in a semi-circle around the propane heater in the stable yard. Amy spread the blankets out on the seats, and they all cocooned in the soft covers. When Laurie arrived, Amy pointed out her chair with the beam of her flashlight, asking, "Isn't this cozy?"

"It's wonderful," Laurie said, slipping into her seat and turning off her light.

As everyone else doused their torches, Grace began to sing. Spider was amazed that such a full, honeyed contralto could come out of that frail-looking body. "Star of the east," she sang. "Thou Bethlehem star."

Ben joined her on the second line. His pure, sweet tenor blended perfectly with hers, creating a rich harmony that tightened Spider's throat again. He reached for Laurie's hand and held it until the last verse soared out into the night.

> *Star of the East, thou hope of the soul,*
> *While round us here the dark billows roll,*

Lead us from sin to glory afar,
Thou star of the East, Thou sweet Bethlehem's star.

When the song was over, Spider remained as he had been during the song, eyes on Amy's creation, Laurie's hand in his. He felt her squeeze his fingers.

"Are you going to read?" she whispered.

"Oh. Yeah."

"I brought out your Bible." Laurie disengaged and handed it to him. "And here's a penlight."

Spider took the small flashlight from her and turned it on. Then he fanned his scriptures open to the New Testament and flipped forward to the book of Luke. Putting the small pool of light on the beginning of Chapter Two, he read, "And it came to pass in those days, that there went out a decree from Cæsar Augustus—"

He stopped suddenly. Looking at Ben's shadowy form to his left, he said, "It starts before that." He paged backward to Matthew.

Now the birth of Jesus Christ was on this wise: When as his mother Mary was espoused to Joseph, before they came together, she was found with child of the Holy Ghost.

Spider read the story to the end, how Joseph had been stricken by the news of Mary's pregnancy and how an angel had appeared and told him to go ahead with the marriage. This was a holy child, the angel said, and Joseph was to be a father to him.

After finishing that chapter, Spider returned to Luke and began again.

With the penlight illuminating each line, he read through the ancient story of Joseph and Mary trying to find a place to stay, ending up in a stable where the baby was born. He read of the shepherds hearing the news from a heavenly choir and making haste to see, looking for a baby wrapped in swaddling clothes and lying in a manger. He finished with the verse about Mary keeping all the things that had happened and pondering them in her heart. Then he turned off the penlight and closed his book.

"Wait!" Amy's voice came from his right. "What about the star? You didn't read about the star."

"That was later, with the three wise men," Laurie said.

"No, Amy's right." Spider turned his flashlight back on. "I should have read about the star." He opened his Bible and, when he had found the passage, read about wise men coming from the east.

When he finished the verse about the star showing where the Christ child was, Amy said, "Read that one again."

Spider obliged.

...and, lo, the star which they saw in the east, went before them, till it came and stood over where the young child was.

Amy sighed. "Can't you just picture it?"

"Your star helps," Spider said. "Now let me finish the next two verses." He read about the gifts of gold, frankincense and myrrh and how the three kings went home by a different way, so they didn't have to report to jealous Herod.

Spider turned off his penlight, and they all quietly contemplated their own star in the east until Grace gave a quick intake of breath. Spider looked at his watch and held it up so Laurie could see the luminous dial. It was eight fifteen.

Laurie turned on her torch and shone it on Grace. "How're you doing?"

Grace seemed to be trying to smile, but it was more of a grimace. "My stitch is back. Boy, it sure is persistent."

Ben rubbed her back. "Do you want to lie down for awhile?" He looked at Laurie. "Would that be all right?"

"Yes. I imagine you'd rather lie down in the house, even if it is dark. You can take your flashlights and one of the lanterns in with you, too, but—"

"But what?" Amy and Ben asked the question at the same time, both sets of eyes wide in the torchlight.

Laurie smiled. "It's nothing to worry about, but this could be the beginning of Grace's labor. It may stay in her back but will probably move around to her belly. When it does, keep track of when the contractions occur, and when they get to be two minutes apart, come and get us."

Ben stood. "Omygosh! Omygosh! Okay." He held up his hands and took a deep breath. "Two minutes. I've got that." He turned to Grace. "Let me help you up. Do you want me to carry you in?"

Grace laughed. "I just made it out to the star and back. I can make it to the house." But she let him help her out of the chair. Still wrapped in her blanket, she walked in the circle of his arm toward the house.

Laurie got up. "I'll go in and see that they're settled." She picked up Ben's blanket. "The house should stay warm for awhile, but I'll take this in just in case. Amy, could you get one of the lanterns from the tack room and bring it in for them?"

Amy stood. "Sure. And then I think I'm going to go to town. I want to see what the star looks like from there."

Spider smiled in the darkness. "I'll bet it looks spectacular."

"I'll bet it does, too." Amy turned on her flashlight and trotted off toward the stable while Laurie followed her own luminous circle to the house.

Spider sat alone, watching her light swinging as she walked. He ran his hand over the cover of his scriptures and sang softly, "Away in a manger, no crib for his bed."

Chapter Nine

WHILE LAURIE WAS getting Grace settled, Spider did some rearranging in the tack room, so he could set up the cots. He carried in the heater, brought in the chairs, and spread the blankets on the cots. The chairs he placed under the window that looked into Goldie's stall.

When everything was set up, Spider cupped his hands around his eyes to block out the lantern light as he pressed against the window and peered into the darkened stall. The palomino restlessly paced a pattern in the sawdust. They might be waiting all night for the foal.

Spider grabbed his flashlight and went to the shop again to search in the darkened storeroom for the place he had stashed the camp equipment. When he found it, he lifted down the camp stove and found the one-gallon coffeepot. He was glad that Jack had put a sink with running water in the tack room.

The pot clanked against the metal of the stove as he left the shop and carried them in one hand, his flashlight in the other.

Laurie opened the stable door as he approached. "If you're trying to sneak up on me, it isn't working," she said, giggling.

"I need more practice." Spider turned off his torch, tossed it on one of the cots, and handed the coffeepot to Laurie. "Would you fill this with water?"

Laurie took hold of the bail. "What're you going to do?"

"I thought you might like some hot chocolate while we're waiting on Goldie." Spider looked around for a surface to put the stove on.

"The stove can go on that bench outside Goldie's stall." Laurie set the pot in the sink and let water stream in. "This is a good idea. I'll go get the cocoa mix and some cookies."

Spider paused at the door. "How many cookies did you make this morning?"

"A couple hundred. I intended to spread them around town this afternoon. That was before the wounded birds and the Bethlehem star." She turned off the tap and followed Spider out the door with the water. Setting the pot on the bench, she turned on her flashlight for her return to the house.

○ʒ

It was well after nine before Spider was finally in his chair with a cup of hot chocolate in his hands. "Aren't you going to sit down and drink yours?" he asked Laurie. "It's going to get cold."

She stood with her forehead against the window, looking into Goldie's stall.

He took a sip. "Is she doing all right?"

"So far. She's still in the first stage. Restless, you know? Down and up. I could use a strong lantern, though. When she finally decides to stay down, I want to be able to see that the foal is presenting properly."

Spider reached over and patted her on the leg. "Have your cocoa, and then I'll go get you one."

Laurie sighed and sat down. "I'm all of a sudden a little tired. Are you?"

"Haven't had time to think about it." He handed her a steaming cup. "It's been quite a Christmas Eve, hasn't it?"

Laurie chuckled. "I can't remember one quite like it."

As she put her cup to her lips, the door burst open.

Ben, eyes wide, stepped through the door, half supporting and half dragging Grace with him.

Spider jumped to his feet and felt Laurie's drink being thrust into his hands as he stared at the young people in the doorway. Neither had on a jacket, and Grace stood spraddle-legged. She was white as a sheet, and Ben was almost as pale.

Laurie was across the room in a second. "What's the matter? What happened?"

Grace began to cry. "It's coming. Oh, Laurie, I can't help it. It's coming. Right now."

Spider set the drinks in the sink. "Right now? How do you know? Haven't you been timing the contractions?"

"Yes, but they never got to two minutes," Ben said. "They kept getting shorter instead."

"Never mind that," Laurie said grimly. "Help me get her on the cot."

Spider and Ben didn't have to be told twice. They picked Grace up and lay her down.

Laurie gave Ben and Spider a list of things to bring from the house, pronto. Ben was out the door in a moment, but Spider paused to ask, "What do you want the paper—"

"Now!" Laurie commanded.

Spider left. He had forgotten his flashlight but didn't want to go back for it, so he depended on the light of Amy's star to find his way to the kitchen door. Luckily, Ben had brought his torch, and he shone it on the counter, so Spider could grab the newspaper and make his way outside. He followed Ben as he dashed back across the pavers to the barn.

Grace was on the cot with her knees up and open. Her formerly pale face was now flushed as she kept her eyes on Laurie and kept repeating, "Hee, hee, hee, hoo."

"You're doing fine, dear," Laurie told her as she pulled a box of latex gloves from the cupboard. "Rest now until the next contraction, and then I'm going to let you push."

Laurie looked at the men, standing just inside the door with their burdens.

"Put your things on one of the chairs," she instructed. "Ben, you're to go to the kitchen and dial 9-1-1. Tell them to send an ambulance. The baby will probably beat them here but tell them to hurry anyway."

Ben nodded and dashed away.

"Spider, my bathrobe is still in the dryer. Will you bring it to me? Take your flashlight this time. And hurry."

Spider saluted, grabbed his torch, and headed for the house again. As he made his way to the laundry room, he heard Ben on the phone.

"What do you mean you can't send anyone?" Ben sounded frantic. "There's a woman here having a baby. She's tiny and frail." There was a pause and then Ben's voce increased in decibels. "No, the *woman* is tiny. The baby isn't here yet."

Spider yanked the dryer door open and dug around for Laurie's bathrobe. He saw a flash of pink, pulled it out, and sprinted to the back door. He reached it just as Ben hung up the phone. Was he crying?

When Spider got to the tack room, Laurie met him at the door. "We haven't much time. Put it on me. Backwards." She stuck out her arms, and when Spider slipped it on her, she turned around, so he could tie it in back. "Is your handkerchief clean? Let me have it."

Spider handed it to Laurie, and she folded it into a triangular shape. As she tied it around her head and underneath her hair, she said, "I'm going to need some dental floss and a pair of scissors. You'll find both in the top drawer in the bathroom. Underneath the sink there's a bottle of rubbing alcohol. Bring that, too."

"I'm on it," Spider said.

As he turned away, he heard Grace say, "Laurie?"

"I'm putting on my gloves, Gracey-love. It's time to get that Christmas baby here."

Spider closed the door behind him and started toward the house. He met Ben at the edge of the patio. "Are they going to send an ambulance?"

"They said the ambulance is out. There was a wreck up north of town. That's what took out the power." Ben's voice cracked. "I said I was going to bring her in myself, and they said don't. They're swamped with injured people from the accident." He took a deep breath and blew it out through his mouth. "They're getting hold of a home health nurse and sending her out."

Spider put his hand on Ben's shoulder. "Buck up, man. Laurie's as good as a home health nurse or a doctor for that matter. Why, she's delivered lots of critters."

"Critters?"

"Calves. Horses. Puppies. The process is the same, man. Grace is in good hands." He took off and called over his shoulder, "I've got to go get stuff for tying the cord."

As he went, he heard Ben mutter, "Critters."

At the house, Spider took the stairs two at a time. He got the things on his list as quickly as he could, though he had to get on his hands and knees to find the alcohol under the sink. Heading back, his torch went out in the upstairs hall. He swore under his breath and made his way gingerly down the stairs.

Ben met him at the bottom. "Laurie says she needs that stuff."

"Already? The baby's here?"

"Can you believe it? C'mon." Ben tugged at Spider's sleeve.

Spider took off, running in the backwash of Ben's light. Slamming through the back door, he sprinted across the pavers to the stable. At the door he skidded to a stop. "Here," he said to Ben. "You take it in."

Ben held up his hands and shook his head. "I'll wait until Grace's ready for me to see her."

Spider opened the door and stepped in. The newborn infant lay on an opened newspaper in front of Grace's flexed legs. The new mother's eyes were closed, but the baby's were open. His arms and legs slowly moved in the air as he took stock of his new world.

"A son," Spider said, smiling. "A little boy."

"He's perfect," Laurie said.

"So why a newspaper?"

"If it hasn't been opened, it's probably the most sterile thing around. I figured I'd be wrapping him in it and sending him on his way in the ambulance. I guess we're going to Plan B." Laurie moved her attention from the baby as Grace's eyes sprang open, and she groaned.

"I'm out of here," Spider said. He opened the door and stepped into the cool, crisp air.

"Is everything all right?" Ben's anxiety showed in his voice.

"Everything's fine," Spider said. "It's a boy."

"A boy?" Ben looked like he was ready to reach for the doorknob.

"They're still busy in there." Spider jerked his head toward the shop. "Let's go see if we can find something to use for a bed."

Ben hesitated for a moment before lighting their way, matching Spider's stride. Halfway to the shop, he said, "About the story you read tonight?"

"Yeah?"

"I've heard it before. Except for that part you read first, about Joseph."

"It gets overshadowed by the shepherds and the star."

"There was something in that story I never realized before."

Spider opened the door to the shop and turned to look at Ben.

"Yeah? What is that?"

"Joseph was a stepfather, too."

Chapter Ten

LATER THAT EVENING, Laurie and Spider sat in the cozy tack room with Grace and Ben and their new little boy. Spider had found a large plastic bin, and Ben had scrubbed and disinfected it while Spider fashioned a mattress out of a foam pad, a towel and a pillow case. The rude bassinet, unused as yet, sat by the cot. Grace held the infant in her arms as she lay propped up on pillows.

Laurie stood at the window, head pressed against the glass as she stared through into Goldie's stall. Spider sat in the chair next to her, facing the young couple.

Ben knelt beside Grace, his head bent over the bundle in her arms. As he touched the tiny hand, the baby's fingers curled around one of his own, and his voice grew husky. "What shall we name him?"

"Noel Latham Clark," Grace said.

Ben smiled at her. "Noel. It's perfect."

Needing something to occupy his attention, so he could give the young couple some privacy, Spider pulled out his pocketknife and picked up a short board he had brought in to block up the baby's bed. Though he kept his eyes on the shavings, he couldn't turn off his ears and was privy to the rest of the murmured conversation.

Grace spoke. "I was hoping we could be married before he came."

"That doesn't matter," Ben said. "I'm his dad whether he comes before or after the wedding."

Trey, sitting outside the stable door, began barking. The baby's arms jerked at the sudden noise, and he began fussing.

Spider put down his whittling and sprang to the door to quiet the dog. As he stepped outside, Grace began to sing a lullaby.

Spider heard the slamming of car doors and peered into the darkness. He saw the corner of the breezeway lighten and then a flashlight beam came floating through. "Is that you, Amy?" he called.

"Shh," Amy replied in a hoarse stage whisper. "Don't say anything."

Spider waited silently for her to approach, and as she neared, he saw she wasn't alone. Two people followed behind her, and through the murky darkness, he could see one of them was shouldering a video camera.

The three paused outside the door as Grace's voice came floating through to them, still singing.

The story was told by the angels so bright,
As round them was shining a heavenly light.
The stars shone out brightly, but one led the way
And stood o'er the place where the dear baby lay.

Amy and the two visitors stood in the light that fell through the high tack room windows and allowed Spider a better view. The young woman with the camera was stocky with short, spiky hair and the glint of metal that must have been a piercing at her lip. The other was tall and willowy with high boots, a short skirt, and long blonde hair topped with a knit beret. She motioned Amy to open the door.

Spider wondered if he should interfere but decided against it. If the ladies were filming a Christmas video, he didn't want to get in their way. He'd keep a close watch, though, to make sure they didn't get pushy.

Amy swung the door wide and then stood blocking the way as she gaped at the sight before her.

Covered with a patchwork quilt, Grace leaned back on the pillows and cradled the baby in her arms. Though both Ben and Laurie looked up when the door opened, Grace kept her eyes on the babe as she sang.

The blonde-haired girl slipped by Amy and whispered something to Ben. He looked at the camera, seemed to consider the request, and then nodded. The blonde motioned the camera closer as Grace sang the last line and then, smiling serenely, raised her beautiful dark eyes to look straight into the lens.

"Cut," said the blonde. She looked at her watch and then spoke to all in the room. "Hi. I'm Claire, and this is Monty. We're students over at Dixie State, and we heard about someone over here hanging a star in the sky. We thought we'd do a segment on it and see if we could get KZUT to pick it up."

Monty took the camera off her shoulder and spoke to Claire. "We don't have much time for editing."

Claire nodded, and her eyes again swept the room. "We'd like to talk to you some more, but right now we've got to see if we can get this on the air." She appealed to Grace. "Is that all right with you?"

Grace's eyes went back to the baby asleep in her arms. "Yes."

Ben added, "His name is Noel Latham Clark."

"Got it," Claire said. "Come on, Monty. We've got work to do." She paused at the door. "We'll be back soon. We can do this in the car."

As the videographers left, Trey began to bark again. Spider watched through the doorway as a momentary halo shone around the house.

Deducing that another car had arrived, Spider called, "We've got more company."

Laurie moved behind him and looked out. "We're not having the whole county traipsing in here to look at this baby."

"They're coming to see the star," Amy said. "You should see it from Kanab."

Spider grinned. "Spectacular?"

Amy grinned back. "More than spectacular. Amazing."

Laurie took hold of the door. "If the whole county is coming up, that's fine. We'll host them, but this little family isn't going to be bothered. They don't need every virus in Kane County being tracked in here."

"Come on, Amy," Spider said, scooting her out the door. "I'll build a fire, so people can warm themselves. You heat up the water for hot chocolate. Laurie, darlin', looks like people decided to come get their cookies since you didn't take them around."

Spider turned to greet the first arrival, a man wearing a gray hoodie. It turned out to be Hank, and Spider enlisted him to help build a fire in the old metal wheelbarrow. They used it for a portable firepit and made some makeshift benches with boards and buckets.

"Don't make the fire too big," Amy said. "I don't want it to overshadow the star."

Hank broke a piece of kindling over his knee. "Nothing could overshadow your star." He pointed with the stick. "Look. You got two more cars coming up the driveway."

Amy practically danced. "It's just like the real Christmas story."

Laurie stepped out of the tack room and called, "We've had another advent."

Spider set down the load of firewood he was carrying. "What?"

"Come and see." Laurie walked to the adjacent stall.

Amy squealed. "Goldie?" She jumped up and down and grabbed Hank, the nearest person, and gave him a hug. "Goldie had her baby."

"Who's Goldie?" Hank asked.

"She's a horse that came to visit." Amy took Hank's hand and dragged him over to join Laurie and Spider at the stable half-door.

Spider shined his light in the stall, and a sorrel colt that seemed to be all legs turned his head to stare at them.

"Oh, look," Amy said. "He's got a star on his forehead."

Laurie put an arm around her. "Another Christmas star."

Spider lowered the beam to the floor. "Can you tell about the hoof?"

"No." Laurie took hold of the top half of the stable door and started swinging it shut. "We need to leave them alone to bond. I'll check to see if it's deformed when I go in later."

"I'll bet it's going to be all right," Amy said. "This is a night made for miracles."

A sound fragment reached Spider's ears, so slight he wasn't sure he had heard anything. "Shhh. Listen," he said. Everyone quieted, and in the silence, there came a faint, "Hello? Anybody home?"

"Someone's at the front door," Amy said, grabbing Hank's hand again. "C'mon. Let's see who it is."

They clattered off, and the darkness swallowed them up. Laurie finished closing the stable door, and Spider latched it. Then he drew Laurie to him. "How're you doing?"

She leaned against his chest, and he felt her warmth as he breathed in her familiar scent.

"I'm fine," she said. "I don't know that I'm ready for more company, though."

Spider kissed her on the top of her head and then heard Amy holler, "It's the home health nurse."

"Thank heavens," Laurie said. "The cavalry has arrived."

Chapter Eleven

SPIDER AND LAURIE walked together to greet the round, grandmotherly woman who slowly came through the breezeway with Amy on one side and Hank on the other.

She introduced herself as Mrs. Kingston and pointed her cane at Amy's creation hanging below the bluff. "I followed your star. It's like Fourth of July frozen in the sky."

Laurie laughed. "It's all Amy's doing. We're very glad it led you here."

"I don't get called out very often. I move a little slow, but I know babies." Mrs. Kingston waved her cane toward the lights of the tack room. "Is that where this new little one is? I'd better go take a look at him and his mother."

"We'll walk you over." As she and Hank continued with the nurse, Amy said over her shoulder, "There was another car pulling in. Better go rescue them."

"I'm on it," Spider said, striding across the pavers and through the breezeway. Rounding a corner, he almost collided with someone. Sensing, rather than seeing, a startled reaction, he heard a familiar voice say, "Spider?"

"Toby? Is that you?"

"Yeah. It's me."

"What're you doing back here? I thought you were up in Panguitch, popping the old question-a-roonie."

Toby's answer was a strange, strangled sound.

Next, Spider felt himself being embraced by a sobbing, inarticulate deputy. Toby was weeping on his shoulder.

Spider patted him on the back, made soothing noises, and hoped that Toby had his own handkerchief.

When the sobbing abated, Spider took him by the shoulders and pushed him back. "Would it help to talk about it?"

He heard Toby blow his nose, farmer style. That solved the handkerchief problem.

"Yes," Toby said damply.

Spider took him by the arm, shining a lighted circle in front of them to follow. "Come over to the fire," he said. "We won't be disturbed. The rest are in with the baby."

"Baby?"

"Yeah. Grace had her baby."

"Really? Where is she?"

"In the barn."

"Really?" Toby tripped over an uneven paver.

"Eyes on the ground," Spider admonished.

They made it the final fifty feet to the wheelbarrow firepit. Spider turned off his lantern and sat on a bench, and Toby plopped down beside him.

"Now," Spider said. "Spill the beans."

"What beans?"

"The girl-in-Panguitch beans."

Toby sighed. His shoulders drooped, and he pulled the ring box out of his jacket pocket and fiddled with the lid. "I guess I won't be needing this."

"Take it back to the store," Spider suggested. "Get your money back."

"Can't. I bought it on Ebay." Toby flipped the lid open, revealing an engagement ring and wedding band. "The diamond's not very big, but I didn't think she was the kind of a girl that would care about that."

Spider picked up a stick and pushed an ember back into the fire. "Did she turn you down flat?"

Toby cleared his throat. "I never got the chance to ask her," he said in a constricted voice. "She'd invited another fellow down from Salt Lake for Christmas. He works in computers."

Spider laid his hand on Toby's shoulder. "Well, we're glad to have you here with us. We've had all kinds of things going on today. Amy's star. Ben and Grace's little boy. And Goldie had a colt."

Toby leaned back, eyes wide. "Goldie? The horse you're keeping for—" He wagged his thumb over his shoulder as if that would supply the missing name.

"Yeah. Cute little sorrel."

"Is his hoof all right?"

"Don't know yet. Laurie wants to give them a chance to bond before she starts invading their space."

"Makes sense." Toby looked at the ring set and sighed. Then he closed the lid and put the box back in his pocket.

Someone called from the breezeway. "Amy? Mr. or Mrs.? Anybody?"

Toby turned toward the sound. "Who's Mr. or Mrs. Anybody?"

"I think she means me." Spider called out, "Over here." He went to light the way, and as he approached, he saw it was the video duo that had arrived earlier. "We're over by the fire," he said. "Did you get your editing done already?"

Monty, the stocky cameraperson, answered him. "The result of good camerawork. We not only got it done, but the boss lady herself is going to look at it.

"You don't say!" Spider led the two women to where Toby stood by the fire. "This is Toby Flint," he said by way of introduction. "Toby, meet Claire and Monty. They're journalism students who heard about Amy's star and came over to see it."

Toby laughed. "Really?" Turning, he asked the girls, "Who told you about the star?"

"My grandma lives here in Kanab," Claire said. "Her neighbor's husband works at the hardware store, and he said some crazy lady came in and said President Obama told her to make a replica of the Bethlehem star."

Toby didn't respond, and in the flickering firelight, Spider read discomfort on his face.

The silence stretched out, and Claire said, "What? Did I say something wrong?"

"Think about it, Claire." Monty's voice had a hint of exasperation in it. "The fact that we're sitting right under the star is a clue that the person who made it lives here." Monty turned to Spider. "The segment is quite nice. Would you like to see it?"

"Sure," Spider said. "How're we going to manage that with the power off?"

"I've got it on my tablet. Let's sit down." She sat on the bench in front of the fire and tapped an arrow on the screen.

Spider sat beside her and watched the image become a lighted street that looked like Kanab. The off-camera narrator—probably Claire—explained that they had heard someone was erecting a star in the vicinity, and they had come to find it. "They said the star was east of Kanab. We're turning now to head that way."

As the car followed the ninety-degree bend at the junction, the brightly illuminated Samco service station went dark along with the rest of the town.

"That's weird," Claire mumbled on camera. "Do they turn off the electricity at nine every night?"

They continued driving east, finally reaching the inky edge of town where the highway climbed a knoll. As they gained the top, they were suddenly able to see a dazzling Christmas-card star low on the eastern horizon.

"Holy Toledo," Claire said in a hushed voice as the car pulled over and stopped.

"Look." It was Monty's voice now on the video. "Some people are out here watching the star." There was the hum of a window going down and then her voice, calling, "Excuse me. Could we talk to you?"

A man in a light-colored hoodie came to the open window. In the darkness, his features were obscured.

The question was Claire's. "What do you know about that star?"

"I know it's spectacular," the man said.

Spider chuckled.

"Who put it up?" Claire asked.

"A very talented individual."

"We heard it was a crazy lady who was saying that President Obama told her to recreate the Bethlehem star."

"Well, I don't know if it was President Obama, but I saw someone in a big, black, stretch limo stop and talk to a friend of mine." He pointed to the star. "Judge for yourself whether she's crazy."

Spider touched Monty on the arm. "Will you play that again? What that fellow said?"

"Sure." She backtracked and played the segment about the crazy lady. "Is that what you wanted?"

"Yeah. Thanks," Spider said. His throat felt tight again, and he had a warm feeling around his heart. Ol' Hank doing his village protection thing. Good man.

"Let's see the rest," Toby said.

Monty tapped the arrow, and the image of the star stayed in the middle of the screen as they traveled up what sounded like a gravel road. Claire's voice became tentative, maybe a little scared, as they drove through the dark, finally reaching the house.

The next scene was a picture of the stable with the star above it, and then the camera approached the door. Spider heard Amy whispering they needed to be quiet, and then she was in the frame, opening the door to the tack room as Grace's voice floated to them singing the lullaby.

Spider sucked in a breath when the camera discovered Grace. She looked like a Madonna, cradling the child in her arms and gazing down upon it as she sang, unaware the lens was recording her every move. She looked up, gazed into the camera, and smiled serenely. Then the screen went dark.

"Wow," Toby said. "Wow."

Monty hugged the tablet to her chest. "Did you like it?"

"It was all great," Toby said. "I'd like to see it again, but I think we've got more visitors. Don't go away."

Spider gave Toby the flashlight. "You're the official greeter." He watched the deputy head toward the breezeway and then turned to Claire. "Can I put you in charge of cookies and hot chocolate?"

Claire agreed, and after Spider showed her where things were, he walked to the firelight's edge to greet the most recent visitors. It turned out to be Bishop Shaefer and his family. Spider shook hands all around, and Toby herded the group over to the benches, so Monty could play the video for them.

Spider walked to the barn and poked his head in the tack room, asking for help with visitors. Hank and Amy came out, and he gave them the task of getting lights out front using some of Amy's unused lights, a battery, and an inverter. When they were gone, Spider stepped inside the cozy stable room.

Grace was sitting up in one of the camp chairs, cocooned in the patchwork quilt. Mrs. Kingston sat beside her with Laurie and Ben occupying the other seats. The baby slept in his makeshift bed sitting atop a bale of hay.

Spider paused to gaze at the tiny new being asleep with one little fist up by his cheek. Laurie joined him, and he put his arm around her waist. "Is that my sock you've got on his head?" he whispered.

"I cut off the top to make a cap. The rest of it is still in your drawer."

"I take comfort in that," he murmured. "By the way, we're getting lots of company out there. What's Bishop Shaefer's wife's name?"

"Are they here? Um, it's Vereen, I think."

"She works in the courthouse, doesn't she? Do you know where?"

"She's the county clerk." She cocked an eyebrow at him. "Why do you want to know?"

Spider winked at her. "Amy said this was a night made for miracles."

Chapter Twelve

As the evening progressed, more and more townspeople arrived. They did a lot of talking about the accident up by Orderville that took out the substation and sent six people to the hospital. But they talked even more about the star. Everyone wanted to tell where they were when they first spied it.

And they talked about the wedding. Spider heard the whispering as the news was passed around. "Vereen went down and opened the office, so they could have a marriage license. Bishop Shaefer's gonna officiate when they get back." He heard cell phone conversations as the news went out over the airwaves. They usually ended with, "Just follow the star."

The more practical minded brought chairs, firewood and portable fire pits, and blankets to wrap up in. Soon the vast paved area behind the house was dotted with groups of people clustered around flickering fires. A child began singing "Away in a Manger," and others joined in.

They had just finished the song when Toby burst through the breezeway hollering, "They're back." He held up his torch to spotlight Vereen and Ben as they came through. Everyone cheered, and Toby announced, "As soon as Bishop Shaefer and the bride are ready, we'll have the—" He broke off and looked up.

The throbbing thwick-thwick-thwick of a helicopter's rotors sounded loudly in the darkness.

Spider scanned the sky to locate it.

A little boy shouted, "There it is!" Everyone turned in the direction he was pointing as the airship became visible over the house.

"I hope he doesn't get too close to that line going to the top of the cliff," Spider muttered.

Laurie asked, "What does it say on the side? KZUT? Did Amy's star make the news?"

The helicopter disappeared behind the house again, and Spider took Laurie's hand and led her through the breezeway. "It may have. Monty sent it in."

They reached the driveway, and they could see the helicopter hovering over the alfalfa field below them. Toby dashed out, hollering, "I'll go light the field for them." He hopped in his car and tore out of the driveway with Hank and Amy right behind him.

"Holy Toledo!"

Spider wheeled around to see who had spoken and found Claire beside him.

"What is it?"

"That's Kathryn Engle, executive producer and powerhouse at KZUT. I've got to get down there."

As Claire held up her cell phone to light her way to her VW, Laurie said, "Kathryn Engle is also Grace's mother. Now the fat's in the fire."

They stood and watched as the two pickups bumped over the field to light a landing area, and the helicopter set down between them.

Laurie linked her arm through Spider's. "Do you suppose she saw the piece Monty sent in?"

"I think it's pretty certain."

"Well, at least she already knows about the baby. How'd she get here so fast?"

"Beats me. She must have been pretty far south doing news things and just came on over when she recognized her daughter." Spider tugged on Laurie's arm. "We'd better go let Grace know her mother'll be at her wedding."

Chapter Thirteen

WHEN THEY TOLD Grace that her mother was on the way up the driveway, she grew pale, and her hand went to her throat. "I don't want to see her until I'm Mrs. Clark," she said, taking Ben's hand.

Laurie looked at Spider. "I vote that you're the one to tell her. I'll stay in here with Grace."

Spider snorted. "Mrs. Kingston can take care of Grace."

"She can't walk out with her for the ceremony," Laurie countered.

"I want Spider to walk out with me," Grace said. "I want him to give me away."

Spider sent a triumphant glance Laurie's way.

Grace added, "But I think he should be the one to tell my mother how things stand."

A knock sounded at the door. "Spider," Toby called. "Kathryn Engle wants to talk to Grace."

Grace's brown eyes were large as she looked up at Spider. He read in them a plea for help, and he sighed. "Okay. Give me five minutes and then let's get this wedding under way." Opening the door just wide enough to slip though, he stepped outside and confronted the powerhouse at KZUT.

She was tall, almost as tall as Spider. Shoulder length blonde hair in an elegant cut framed a handsome face with a jaw that seemed set. She had the same large eyes as

Grace, but hers were steel gray and looked like they had had a lot of practice in seeing through subterfuge.

"Good evening, Ma'am. I'm Spider Latham. I'm, uh. . ." He looked around at the crowd gathered in the back yard, many of them staring at the woman who had come in a helicopter. "Let's talk someplace else."

He led her along Hank and Amy's luminous path through the breezeway and out onto the front drive. With the beam of his flashlight, he indicated the low wall that ran along the far side. "Would you care to sit a minute?"

She didn't sit. "Don't think you can charm me with your aw-shucks, Jimmy Stewart imitation," she said in clipped accents. "I've come to get my daughter and take her home."

Spider turned off his flashlight and gazed up at Amy's star, searching his mind for something to say. Trying to defuse her anger, he said, "Home means different things to different people."

"Home is home." Her voice allowed no opposition.

"Yeah, but if it turns out that home's not a safe place, then maybe it becomes something else."

"What are you saying?" Her voice cut through the darkness like a switchblade.

"The Princeton man? The one you insisted she go out with?"

Silence.

She finally sat on the wall.

When she spoke, all the steel had gone out of her voice. "I did this to her."

"Good things are coming from it, Mrs. Engle. Ben's a good man, and she loves him."

She sniffed but said nothing.

Spider went on. "Ben will raise the boy as his own. He's studying to be an electrician, and he'll be able to provide for her well."

"An electrician." She spoke as if she had bit into something bitter. "I wanted her to marry a lawyer."

Spider turned on his flashlight and swept it in an arc over the valley below. "Earlier this evening there were lights scattered all over down there. You could see the lights of Kanab over by that point. Right now, who do you think those people would rather see? An electrician or a lawyer?"

More silence. Then a sigh. "All right." Finally, she stood. "When I got here, people were talking about a wedding. I understand the bride is my daughter."

"Yes. Shall we go? It's about to start." Spider led her back through the breezeway. Halfway to the festive back yard, she linked her arm through his and said, "I insist on a front row seat."

Chapter Fourteen

SPIDER AND LAURIE waved to the last of their guests, and he put his arm around her as they walked back to the benches where Amy sat alone.

Spider threw another log on the fire and stood watching it begin to burn. "What an evening!"

"It was a magical night," Laurie said. "I think the most magical time was when Bishop Shaefer asked about a ring, and Toby pulled that little box out of his pocket."

He chuckled. "Yeah, ol' Toby. He did all right."

Hearing a door close, Spider looked toward the barn and saw a light coming toward them. When it got closer, he recognized Ben and his new mother-in-law.

"Mrs. Kingston is helping Grace with Noel's feeding," Ben said. "We thought we'd come out here and wait." He paused while Mrs. Engle took a seat and then sat on a different bench.

"How is Grace doing?" Laurie asked. "Did the wedding tire her out?"

"A little, but she's doing fine." Ben held his hands to the fire. "And your colt? Did you check his hoof?"

"I did." Laurie smiled. "He's perfect."

At that moment, the lights flickered and came on. The halogen on top of the garage and the one on top of the barn cast shimmering circles that intersected where the little group sat around the fire. The windows of the house glowed in the dark, spilling light out onto the patio in golden trapezoidal bricks.

"Ooooh," Amy moaned. "The magic is gone."

"Well, the magic may be gone, but the furnace is on, and we'll have a warm place to sleep tonight." Laurie stood. "Mrs. Engle, may I show you to your room? I hope you won't mind sharing with Mrs. Kingston. You'll have twin beds, and it's right next to Grace and Ben's room."

Ben got up. "I'll come with you. If Mrs.—I mean Mother Engle—wants to shower, I'll carry the water out for her."

Mrs. Engle paused and looked from Laurie to Spider, a frown on her face.

"We've got drain problems," Spider said. "Ben will explain about all the complications."

"And he'll show you where the porta-potty is," Amy added.

Mrs. Engle stared at Spider for a moment, and then a smile lifted the edges of her mouth. "I suppose you're going to ask me whether I'd rather see a plumber right now or a lawyer?"

Spider answered her smile. "It crossed my mind."

Mrs. Engle looked up at Amy's star and then reached her hand out to her son-in-law. "Come with me, Ben, and show me what you're worth."

Spider watched them walk hand in hand toward the house behind Laurie. "You got it right, Amy. It's a night made for miracles."

ABOUT LIZ ADAIR

A native of New Mexico and mother of seven, Liz Adair bloomed late as a writer. Though she lived in green, moist, northwest Washington State for forty years, many of her books are set in the southwest.

Liz returned to high plateau country in 2012 when she and her husband, Derrill, moved to Kanab, Utah. Liz had gone to high school in Kanab and neighboring Fredonia, Arizona, so moving there was like coming home. It was natural for her next book to be another Spider Latham mystery, even though ol' Spider hadn't inhabited one of her books for ten years. Writing about him again felt like coming home, too, and a Christmas story at the Latham's was like Christmas with an old friend.

Liz was widowed in 2025 and returned to Washington to live with her daughter, Terry Gifford. Together they have a YouTube channel, *Red Falcon Road* based out of Willowbrook Manor, Terry's English Teahouse and Farmstay

Liz has her own corner of Willowbrook's newsletter, so if you'd like to follow her there, go to www.teaandtour.com and subscribe to *The Willowbrook Word*.

OTHER BOOKS BY LIZ ADAIR

Trouble at the Red Pueblo, a Spider Latham Mystery set in Kanab

Death on the Red Rocks, a Spider Latham Mystery set in Kanab.

The McCarran Collection, a romantic suspense set in Kanab.

The Lodger, a Spider Latham Mystery

After Goliath, a Spider Latham Mystery

Snakewater Affair, a Spider Latham Mystery

The Mist of Quarry Harbor, a romantic suspense set in the San Juan Islands of Washington State.

Cold River, a romantic suspense set in northwest Washington State.

Interlude at Cottonwood Spring, historical fiction based on family history and set in New Mexico during the Great Depression

Hidden Spring, a novella in the *Timeless Romance, Old West Collection*, also available as a standalone.

Letters from Afghanistan, a compilation of Liz's mother's letters written from Afghanistan, 1965 to 1970.

No-Town Girl: A Memoir, due out in November 2025

Grandma Tudy's Kitchen, a cookbook due out in March 2026

The Hayride
A Short Story

by

Ron Shook

THE HAYRIDE

RICKIE LOOKED AROUND him at the living room of his new home. New home, new town, new school. He was seated on the floor with his back against the tan microfiber couch. All around him, wherever he looked he saw the clutter of a successful Christmas morning. His mother had tried to keep up with the flood of wrapping paper, wadding each piece up and putting it up in a garbage bag, but the sheer volume overwhelmed her as presents were not so much unwrapped as torn apart. Finally, she had just gone with the flow, sitting on the couch and watching bemusedly as her brood gleefully shredded paper. Santas were torn limb from limb, candles were sundered, candy canes, snowflakes, pine trees, cute little bears, and the occasional angel were all turned to confetti.

But the feeding frenzy had died down. Now, his sister Annie was modeling a sweater she'd pulled on over her new Christmas pajamas. His other sister Bobbie wore identical new pajamas, as did all the members of the family. The PJ's were a Christmas tradition. Starting in November, Rickie's mother spent hours at the sewing machine, making pajamas for all the family members. Each year was a theme. Last year it had been clowns. This year it was convicts.

Rickie's dad was idly turning the crank of a new spinning reel; Bobbie was deep into a new book. Rickie turned to his mother. "So, is that all?" It was an old joke. His mother smiled, a brief twist of the lips. A very old joke.

Rickie looked out through the big picture window at the bright morning sunshine that highlighted the red sandstone cliffs at the edge of town. He knew that if he stepped outside in his pajamas, he'd feel a little chill, just a slight nippiness. He might curl the toes of his bare feet. But the cold would be gone in an hour, chased away by the rising sun. Christmas day and the temperature was predicted to be in the 60s.

In his mind's eye Rickie pictured a world without snow anywhere on Christmas Day. There would be groups singing carols in shorts and tee shirts, candy canes hanging from palm trees, Santa in a sleigh with wheels. Would it really be Christmas without any snow at all, anywhere? At least he could imagine a place where it was snowy. What if no one had ever seen snow at all? What would that be like? Maybe there wouldn't be any Christmas anywhere.

The sounds of his family receded and Rickie became enmeshed in his thoughts and fancies. His father always said that he was "going walkabout," but his sisters called it "zoning." Sometimes his "walkabout" sessions lasted a few seconds; sometimes he would stay in them until yanked out. His mother said she worried about his mental state.

"Hey Zono!" Bobbie spoke loudly enough to penetrate Rickie's thoughts. "What'cha dreaming of?" Bobbie didn't have patience with Rickie's absences from family gatherings or, for that matter, with the reputation he was getting among his teachers for daydreaming in class.

Rickie jerked upright. "Snow!" he said, louder than he needed to.

There was a short silence then everybody laughed. Rickie blushed, as he always did when caught in a trance. "I mean, no snow," he said. "In Soda Springs there'll be a foot in the front yard and it'll be ten below zero. It's just not right. Christmas is about snow. Y'know, Sleigh bells jinglin' and all that stuff. Building snowmen." He pointed out the window, "All this sunshine, Christmas isn't any different from any other time of year."

Bobbie snorted. 'You mean you'd rather have below? You are out of your mind."

"No, though I don't mind the cold. Not like some wimpy people I know. It's just that it doesn't seem like Christmas without snow."

Mother said, "Christmas isn't about snow. It's about…"

"PRESENTS!" shouted Annie and Bobbie in unison.

Offended, mother was about to give a strong lecture on the Meaning of Christmas, when they were interrupted by a loud, prolonged pounding on the door.

Mother shook her head. "That will be the Jones boy. He doesn't believe in doorbells."

"He doesn't know how they work," sniffed Bobbie.

Rickie sprang up and went to the door, opening it to admit not only the Jones boy, William by name, but three other people. Will Jones bounded into the room, radiating a kind of undirected but boundless energy. He was a round-faced young man of Rickie's age, sixteen, with his hair parted in the middle and worn rather long. Winter and summer he wore the same thing: jeans and t-shirts with obnoxious slogans on them. Today it was "Nuke the whales" in honor of Christmas.

"Hey Stinson family, Merry Christmas," he boomed as his eyes darted around, looking for a candy dish or two. "Aren't you glad you're in good ol' warm Kanab instead of Soda Pop Springs? I saw on the weather channel that it's twelve below up there. Cold enough to freeze your…," his voice trailed off as he saw Mrs. Stinson's eyebrows rise. "You'll freeze," he finished.

Will stopped talking. He'd just taken in the pajamas. "What's going on?" he asked. "Y'all look like referees."

Mrs. Stinson was affronted. "We're convicts, not referees."

Seeing that his mother's explanation wasn't helping, Rickie explained. "We get new pajamas every Christmas. This year, they look like convict uniforms."

Will was incredulous. "You sleep in pajamas?" He looked around, at the girls and especially at Rickie's parents. "All of you?" He shrugged. "Well, it takes all kinds. I don't sleep in anything at all, myself."

This brought a burst of giggling from the three people behind him. Will turned, as if remembering them for the first time. "These are cousins of mine from Orderville. Soup eaters one and all. We're all related somehow or another, cousins most likely. They've come to the big city for the day."

Mr. Stinson broke in. "What's all this about soup eating?"

Will explained, "Early settlers in Orderville began to practice the United Order, kind of Communism with Jesus. Legend has it that they made big pots of soup that everybody dipped from."

"Ah," Mr. Stinson said. "And that's where the name Orderville comes from. I wondered about that."

"Yeah," Will said. "The experiment didn't last long, but the name stuck."

"Look," Will said, addressing the three Stinson teens. "You're new here and maybe miss Soda Springs this Christmas. So, we've come to cheer you up and show you a whole new way to celebrate Christmas. Up there, you probably go for a sleigh ride on Christmas Day. Well, down here we do it differently. We go for a—pause with drum roll—HAY RIDE. Yayyy!" And he waved his arms like a circus announcer.

There was a stunned silence. Finally, Mrs. Stinson asked tentatively, "Hay ride?

Will nodded. "See, my uncle Slim has a tractor and a trailer. He uses it to haul hay. Every now and again we toss a couple of hay bales on it, get a gang of kids together, and go for a ride."

Rickie asked, "Where do you go?"

"Anywhere we want to. We just take off cross-country, and as long as we don't fall into a canyon or tip over, we can go anywhere. Don't even need a road. What do you say? Come on and have a real Kanab Christmas. Forget about cold and snow." Will turned to Mr. and Mrs. Stinson. "You are welcome to come along too. It'll be really dull and boring, though."

"You're sure it's safe?" asked Mrs. Stinson, who seemed ready to think that it probably wasn't.

"Sure. We've done it lots of times, and no one has ever gotten hurt. Not seriously."

"C'mon, Mom. We'll be fine," said Rickie. He turned to his sisters. "Coming?"

"No." "Yes." Bobbie wouldn't go and Annie would. Bobbie pointed at her new book as if that was all that needed to be said.

Dressed for the southern Utah dead of winter, jeans, tennis shoes, a shirt and a light jacket, the two Stinsons trooped out with the other kids and hopped into a minivan with Will driving, and off they went, into the clear, warming day.

Rickie was feeling a little disoriented, as if he were viewing a movie of himself riding in the minivan, only he was sitting at the back of a large theater. He could hear, he would participate, but he wasn't really *there*. Part of him was in Soda Springs, Idaho, where it would be cold outside and warm inside. There would be a fire in the fireplace, and if you went outside you bundled up good and didn't touch anything metal with bare hands, and you didn't run too much or you'd frost your lungs, and you played basketball outside in huge mittens and snowmobile boots. The snow and the cold made the season real. The snow on the trees was real, not fake, and the icicles were real, and you could break one off and suck clean cold water out of it. Santa dressed in fur trimmed wool and had a long beard because he had to, so he didn't freeze. When you sang "Silent Night," you thought of a small village deep in snow, a clear, cold night with full moon overhead and one bright star, the smoke curling out of chimneys in houses with snow up to the windowsills. The hooves of the reindeer landing on the roof were muffled by snow, and the trees were all pines or firs.

But this—Rickie looked out at the red rocks and the green juniper trees and the blue sky—this wasn't Christmas country. This was a clownsuit country, with its garish hues and lapis lazuli sky. Purple rock. Whoever heard of purple rock? How could the Christ child come to a house made of sandstone slabs? And the manger scene in the town square? You stood in front of it and behind, all around, were bright vermillion mesas dotted with juniper and stunted cedar. There was no sense of peace there. No serenity.

He was brought into the here and now by a sudden jolt, as the minivan skidded to a stop in a dirt parking lot somewhere north of Kanab. Rickie wasn't quite sure where they were, because he hadn't been paying attention. He looked around.

To his left were red sandstone hills dotted with cedar and juniper trees. The same to his right. Ditto straight ahead of him.

He turned. Just behind him was the road, and, across the road…red sandstone hills dotted with cedar and juniper trees. The only different feature was a road that led out of the parking lot into a cleft in the hills.

Parked at the beginning of the road was an old John Deere tractor hitched to a flat wagon about sixteen feet long and maybe eight feet wide. The bed of the wagon came up to his jeans' pocket. He could turn his back to it, hop a little and be sitting on it. Three hay bales sat atop the wagon arranged in a triangle.

Rickie walked around the whole lash-up, a dubious expression on his face. The John Deere was idling quietly, a faint *chuff chuff chuff* coming from the exhaust pipe.

Another car pulled in the lot and more kids piled out. At a quick count, Rickie came up with twelve people. He knew a few of them, but most were strangers. More kids from Orderville? Or from Fredonia to the south?

Will jumped up on the trailer bed and whistled a loud two-finger whistle that Rickie couldn't do and wished he could. "Hey everybody," he shouted. "Let me introduce," he looked around, "Rickie," pointing, "and Annie," pointing. "They are from the frozen north, and we're going to thaw them out." He laughed, delighted with his own wit.

"Now," he said, "Pile on. The train is leaving."

Everybody, girls and guys alike, wore jeans and sturdy shoes with light jackets or sweatshirts. They'd obviously done this before. "Well," Rickie thought, "If they can do it, so can I." He flopped his bottom on the wagon bed, hitched his legs on and stood up. He looked for Annie and saw Will handing her onto the wagon. She smiled a shy thanks. Most of the guys and some of the girls just jumped on, using strong young legs to haul themselves up.

Will clambered up onto the seat of the tractor and pushed the throttle lever forward a bit. The *chuff chuff chuff* changed to a deeper *chug chug chug*. Will pushed a lever forward and the tractor abruptly took off at a brisk walk. A couple of boys on the end weren't ready and were dumped off the wagon into the soft dirt of the parking lot. Laughing, they stood up, took two or three running steps and jumped back on the wagon.

The John Deere chugged on.

They navigated the road up through the gap in the hills, the kids joshing each other and getting acquainted with

Rickie and Annie. Rickie learned that about half of the kids were from Fredonia, a small town seven miles south and over the state line in Arizona. He also learned that, in some way or another, most of the people were related to each other. One of the guys, a Fredonia boy named Fred Swapp, told Rickie that he had to be careful when he fell in love with a girl. "A couple times I got a crush on a cousin," he explained. "Can't do that. I've had family break my heart more than anyone else. You're lucky. You're from outside. You can date anyone you want to. Except your sisters. But you gotta' know, everybody in the valley can date *them,* so they'll be right popular."

At the time, Rickie and Fred were sitting on the back of the trailer, legs dangling off the end. Suddenly, the wheels of the trailer went over a bump in the road, the rear of the wagon flipped up, and Rickie and Fred were thrown off the end of the wagon and landed on their seats in the middle of the road. The dirt in the road was soft, and the landing had been light, so Fred, followed by Rickie, still a little dazed, jumped up, ran to the trailer and leapt on, only to be pushed off again by one of the other boys. Rickie, possibly because he was the new kid in town, was not bothered as he scrambled on again. Breathless, he walked swaying to one of the hay bales and sat down on it.

He noticed that a number of contests were developing among the boys and some of the girls on the trailer. They would see how far they could walk along the 3-inch-wide metal strip that was the wagon edge before they fell off. Laughing, they'd jump back on and try it again. One of the girls, who walked like a gymnast, made it nearly halfway around the circumference before she fell.

Others would ride the wagon bed as if it were a surfboard, standing sideways and trying to keep their feet in one place. One boy fell off into a cactus and spent the next twenty minutes picking spines out of his leg.

Some couples were just sitting on bales holding hands.

Rickie saw Will sitting next to Annie. *Wait a minute*, he thought. *Who's driving the tractor?* He turned to look. Up front, the John Deere chugged along, steering wheel yawing slightly, as it slowly moved across the valley floor with no one at the wheel at all.

Will saw him staring at the driverless tractor and waved a hand. "S'all right. Doesn't matter where we go, so we don't need to steer it. Relax and enjoy yourself."

Rickie stood and looked at the landscape. All around was level ground, dotted with small sagebrush, bunch grass, and tumbleweeds. The swaying of the wagon, the laughter of the guys and girls, the *chug chug chug* of the tractor, all had a soothing effect, almost hypnotic, almost…

Rickie imagined a Christmas without presents. Would it be Christmas then? He imagined a family sitting around the tree in the morning. What would they do? Tell stories? Play, "I'm thankful for…?" No that was thanksgiving.

So Christmas was about presents. It was the one thing that was universal to Christmas. Even the things we normally think about when we think of Christmas weren't universal. Christmas was very popular in Japan, Rickie had been told, and they weren't celebrating the birth of Jesus. They didn't believe in Jesus. Besides, Jesus wasn't born in December; he was probably a spring baby. The Christmas tree was added much later, and not everybody had Christmas trees. In Hawaii, they decorated palm and banana trees.

It was presents. Bobbie and Annie had been right that morning. Mom would say it's about giving, but that's only the other end of the equation. If giving is on the one side, getting is on the other. Or maybe Christmas is about the whole equation—giving and getting. Trying to figure out what the other person wants. And being happy or sad with what you get.

Rickie gradually became conscious of the people around him. They were quieter now, less inclined to horseplay. Their earlier energy had burned off, and now they were quietly enjoying the ride, the swaying and occasional jouncing of the trailer, the chug of the tractor motor, the silence of the day. He felt relaxed and content, leaning against one of the hay bales, his feet dangling off the trailer. There was a lot to be said for Christmas in a warm climate.

"Hey!" shouted a voice from near the end of the trailer, "Aren't we near the petroglyphs? Let's go see 'em."

A chorus of "Yes," and "Let's do," and "Right," echoed the speaker.

Will was annoyed; Rickie could tell. He was involved in getting to know Annie. She said something softly to him. He nodded with energy, sprang up, gave her his hand and led her up to the front of the wagon, over the wagon tongue, and onto the tractor. Seating himself, he put her on his lap and began to steer a large curve toward the sandstone cliffs to the north about a quarter of a mile away.

The cliffs themselves were nearly vertical bluffs deeply scored by water and smoothed by wind. They were almost bare of vegetation, and long stretches were sandstone slabs overlaid by a black layer. Rickie wondered what the black could be. Oxidation, perhaps? Where the sandstone showed through the black over-layer it shone a brilliant vermillion in the sun.

"Does anybody know anything about these petroglyphs?" Rickie asked the wagon at large.

A girl sitting next to him answered. "My geology teacher says they are about a thousand years old. They were made by either the Fremont peoples or the Anasazi. There are a lot of petroglyphs around here, but not many people know about this one. Even the four-wheelers don't come out here."

Anasazi. The word had an exotic ring that Rickie loved.

He said it a couple of times. It rolled off his tongue in a pleasing rhythm, and with the hard Z at the end, rang with authority.

He turned to the girl. "Thank you," he said. "I'm Rickie, but you know that."

She smiled. "And I'm JaNel. From Fredonia." She was the girl who made it halfway round the wagon rim. She had the tall rangy look of a runner, with short blondish hair and a few freckles across the bridge of the nose. He eyes were blue and set wide. All in all she was very nice indeed.

"Janel?" Rickie asked.

She sighed. "*Capital J, a, n, capital N, e, l.* My grandfather was named James Nelson. He was killed in Vietnam. I'm named after him."

"Ah," said Rickie. "They took the first part of his full name and put them together. It's good that they didn't decide to use the last parts of his name. Then you'd have been, let's see, MesSon."

JaNel laughed. Then she turned thoughtful. "I've been watching you. Sometimes you get real quiet and kind of go away for a while. What are you thinking about?" She touched his arm quickly, "Or is that too personal?"

Blushing, Rickie shook his head. "No, it's okay. My family calls it 'zoning.' I just get to thinking about things and forget about the world around me. I'm sorry."

"No, no," she said. "Don't apologize. What were you thinking about?"

"Christmas."

"Well, this is the time for it. Anything in particular about Christmas?"

Rickie sighed. He liked this girl. But, she had asked. "I was thinking that there's not really anything in this Christmas gig. Nothing I can think of seems to be a valid reason for Christmas. I loved Christmas in Soda Springs— that's in Idaho—when I was young, because it fit the idea I had about Christmas. You know, snow tree in the front room, gifts." He made a gesture at the bright world around him. "This all seems so artificial. No, not artificial, just—staged."

He looked at her apprehensively, but she only nodded, her eyes warm.

Rickie went on, "Did you ever go on a motor trip across the desert in New Mexico or Arizona? You know, you see a big billboard that says, *Buffalo Bill's Trading Post*, and it lists all the wonderful things that are there, like a petting zoo, and Native American goods and moccasins and tomahawks and spears and beaded vests. Then, when you finally get there, you find a run-down collection of shacks with a few cheap trinkets and one or two mangy goats to pet. Well, Christmas is sort of like that to me."

He sat back, suddenly exhausted. He'd never before said aloud what he was thinking.

JaNel didn't say anything.

Rickie chewed his lip. "You think I'm a nut, don't you?"

"Maybe," JaNel said. "But a nice nut." And she took his hand.

They were holding hands when the tractor pulled up sharply in front of a sandstone cliff fronted by a shallow talus slope.

The *chug chug* of the tractor engine went back to a *chuf chuf*. Will jumped down from the driver's seat, helped Annie down, though she didn't need it, and turned to the people on the wagon. "There's kind of a trail off to the left there that leads around that projection," pointing to a jutting cliff face. "You go around it, and the petroglyphs are on your right. I mean, right there, where you can touch them and everything."

Suddenly eager, Rickie hopped off the trailer and turned to help JaNel. She took his hand graciously, though they both knew she didn't need it, and started off up the slope, hand in hand. Soon, though, they had to travel single file. The talus slope was treacherous, piled with loose rock that could turn underfoot and give a pretty severe ankle twist. At the top of the slope, Rickie waited for JaNel.

As she came up beside him, he turned to look at the cliff face just to his right.

He was transfixed. The rock face was covered in excised designs to a height of about eight feet, and along the cliff for perhaps twelve feet. He could recognize some shapes. There were several that were clearly elk, and some others that could have been antelope, perhaps sheep. Some figures were human, while others sported wings and held bows and arrows. There were spirals and curves that could have been snakes. There were patterns of dots, zigzags, and more or less random curves. All had been patiently chiseled into the rock with some primitive tool, perhaps a rock or a piece of antler.

The red sandstone had a thick patina of black over it, and the artists had removed the upper layer of black to let the red show through. The results were dramatic.

Rickie stepped closer to the petroglyphs. Off to his right, near the edge of the panel, he saw what could have been the artist's signature—a palm print in red. It hadn't been incised; it had been painted on. Probably, Rickie thought, the artist had placed his palm in some sort of paint and pressed it against the wall.

On impulse, Rickie stepped up to the wall, reached out, and placed his own palm against the palm print on the rock.

The rock was cool in the midday sun, and the air around Rickie seemed to darken slightly, as if a cloud had come in front of the sun. The rock face in front of Rickie changed, grew translucent, and it seemed to Rickie that he could see into the rock, could follow the line of a wrist and an arm leading from the painted handprint, leading to a young man in the rock. He was Ancestral Puebloan, standing in leather pants and moccasins, a bow in his other hand, an odd-shaped soft cap on his head. He was looking out straight at Rickie.

"Oh-kay," Rickie said to himself. "I'm having a whatchamacallit—hallucination—here." He removed his hand from the handprint and the image of the young Puebloan disappeared. Rickie thought he saw a look of disappointment on the boy's face, but maybe that was his imagination too.

Cautiously, as if it might burn him, Rickie touched the palm print.

Again, there was a slight darkening of the day, and the young man appeared. It was as if Rickie were looking at the other boy through a sheet of darkly tinted glass. "Through a glass darkly," came a random thought into Rickie's mind, and he wondered briefly where it came from.

The young man held a rabbit in his left hand. Perhaps he had shot it with an arrow or captured it in a snare. He held the rabbit out to Rickie, offering it to him.

"Rickie?" A tentative voice at his side. "Are you okay?"

Rickie snapped back to the here and now.

It was JaNel, and she looked worried. "You were standing so still, I didn't even know if you were breathing."

Rickie gave a little embarrassed laugh. "Sorry. I zoned. I was thinking about whoever made that handprint, and I just got caught up in my thoughts."

JaNel looked at him for a moment then nodded. "I like that in you. I think."

But Rickie knew he hadn't zoned. He'd seen something. Back on the trailer, leaning against the hay bale, JaNel's hand in his, he thought about it. A young man offered him a present. Across who knows how many centuries. *I give you a present. I am connected to you, and I show it with a present.*

So that was it. Christmas was about being connected to

people. All the other things were like tinsel on the tree. Rickie thought, *I am connected. To my family. To JaNel here. To my ancestors and to my children, if I ever have any. To the young man who put his handprint on the rock face.*

Another thought popped into his head, and it seemed so right that he decided to share it.

He turned to JaNel. "I just figured out why I have been so grumpy about Christmas. It's because I didn't want to move from Soda Springs. I had friends back there. I was comfortable. So, I've been taking it out on the weather and the countryside. But now, everything is okay." He looked down at their interlocked hands, "More than okay."

He sat up and looked at the landscape around him again. But now it was different. Whereas before he had seen red hills and blue sky, he now saw how the wind and water had sculpted fantastic forms in the cliff faces. He saw how the rock wasn't a uniform red, but varied in shades from orange to vermillion, streaked through with white. He felt the intensity of the blue in the sky, the wistfulness of the few clouds on the horizon.

He sighed. For the first time since he had moved to Kanab, he really *saw* his surroundings, and he felt right at home.

He leaned back against the hay bale and turned to JaNel. "Merry Christmas"

"Hey, Rick." It was Will. "What'cha think of the pictures? Neat-O Bandito, no? And did you like the red hand on the bottom right? I did that myself with some red paint. Sort of a secret signature."

He gave Rickie a friendly slap on the leg and walked up to the tractor, whistling.

About Ron Shook

Ron Shook is recently retired from a nearly 50-year stint as a teacher of non-fiction writing at the university level and is eagerly embarking on his next career as a writer of fiction. He lives with his wife, Mary, in Ogden, Utah, and is a frequent visitor to Southern Utah.